I woke screaming that time. It took about ten minutes before I was really back into my body again—before I was me, myself, Meg Frazer, in a muck sweat, ice cold and trembling in my big comfortable bed. The dream's terror slowly receded, uncurling its grip on me tendril by tendril, leaving only its aftermath, like the acrid smell after a fire—vague memory of pain and falling; sharp, particular memory of the face.

"This can't be borne," somebody stammered in a hoarse, shaky voice. Presently, I understood that it was my own voice. Oddly, this steadied me, because I realized that what it said was true. Such a state of affairs could go on no longer. Something had to be done.

JOAN AIKEN is the well-known author of many successful books for young readers, including *The Wolves of Willoughby Chase, Black Hearts in Battersea, Nightbirds on Nantucket, The Stolen Lake, The Cuckoo Tree, Dido and Pa,* and *The Shadow Guests,* all available in Dell Yearling editions, and *Died on a Rainy Sunday,* available in a Dell Laurel-Leaf edition. Ms. Aiken lives in Petworth, England.

Night Fall

JOAN AIKEN

Published by
Dell Publishing
a division of
The Bantam Doubleday Dell Publishing Group, Inc.
1 Dag Hammarskjold Plaza
New York, New York 10017

Night Fall

THE DAY I MET GEORGE WAS ONE OF THE WORST IN MY life. Not the very worst: that had been three weeks earlier when Mother and Ralph were killed in a car accident on Sunset Boulevard.

I suppose there must have been the usual headlines in the papers about it—they were both movie stars—but I was too young then to know about that, only nine, and much too miserable to care. Ralph was my stepfather, not my real father (whom I could hardly remember at that time), but he was kind, and fun, called me silly names like Popsypetal, and took me on innumerable treats. While Mother was Mother, beautiful, and unpredictable, and irreplaceable.

We had been living in Los Angeles for three years. I couldn't remember a lot about life in England before that, but although I loved the California heat, and our big, white, Spanish-style house, and the friendly, casual American children, I suppose I still felt, in a way, that I was foreign, English, and didn't properly belong in that world. But Mother was always reassuringly there, with her warm teasing voice, and honey-red hair, and her irresistible view that life was marvelous: a symbol of security until the day her convertible was rammed by a truck with faulty brakes, until that noontime telephone call struck away the props of my whole existence.

1

I can still call up the image of Sanchie, the hired girl, staring at me with round, shocked eyes while she talked and listened, and the faces of neighbors who had heard a local newscast and came in with ghoulish, well-meaning sympathy and whispers not meant for my ears.

"Poor little mite, not a soul belonging to her in this continent, who's going to look after her?"

I was too stunned and disbelieving to pay attention at the time, but the words came back later to haunt me.

A Mrs. van Hefflin who lived up the avenue took me to stay with her for a couple of days and in the midst of her noisy lively family I existed in a state of shock, hardly aware of the barbecues and picnics and trips to amusement parks that they kindly organized in the hope of distracting me.

Then my future was arranged, very simply, really: my own father sent a cable from England, I was put on a plane in charge of an elderly married couple who were traveling to London and my new life began.

I heard them say afterward it had been a bumpy trip, but I neither noticed nor worried. Mr. and Mrs. Strangeways were plainly unused to children and, after a few inquiries as to how I was feeling, which I answered in choked mutters, they, probably wisely, left me alone.

People put meals in front of me and took them away again. I tried on my life jacket, fastened and unfastened my safety belt when told to, all the time hardly conscious of what was happening. All I could think of was that Mother was dead, that I should never see her again, never hold her warm hand or kiss her good night or watch her dressing for a party and hear her wonderful, bubbling, golden laugh—that effervescently happy sound which had been the origin of her nickname, Fizz.

"Fizz, are you ready, honey?" Ralph would shout up the stairs. "Better get cracking or we'll be late for the premiere."

"Just saying good night to Meggie, I'll be right down——" and she'd hug me again while we went through the nightly ritual:

"Sleep well! Sweet dreams!"

"Same to you!"

"Same to you!"

"Same to *you*, and many of them."

But there wouldn't be many of them now. There wouldn't be any, ever again.

Faintly, through my fog of misery, I wondered about Father. It had been four years since I saw him last—almost half my lifetime. I could only dimly remember a gray-haired, gray-faced, tired-looking man, much older-seeming than Mother. He had hardly been at home anyway; during most of the time I could remember he was away at the Korean War, and when he did come back it was important not to disturb him.

"Hush, don't make a noise, you'll worry Father, he's not well."

"Why isn't he well? What's the matter with him?"

"He was in a prison camp where the people starved him, so we mustn't be noisy or troublesome because he's very tired and ill."

Perhaps Mother found this state of affairs as hard to adjust to as I did? I couldn't remember anything more about Father; it must have been pretty soon after this that she took me off to America and I presently learned that Ralph was to be my new step-father.

3

With a chill of apprehension, I wondered if I should know Father when I saw him? Whether he would be glad to see me? What he did for a living. And—another thought, more dismaying still—if he had married again. I had read enough stories about wicked stepmothers to know what *that* would mean.

Presently, I fell into a troubled sleep.

It was nine o'clock at night when we reached the London plane terminal. I had a cold, sick, trembling sensation inside me as I stared about at the hurrying people, none of whom resembled my memory of Father. Nobody looked at me or seemed interested. Supposing he hadn't bothered to come and meet me? Supposing he didn't *want* me? Had he been angry when Mother went off and left him, I wondered? Had he missed her then as much as I was missing her now? It was the first time such a thought had occurred to me.

Then a woman detached herself from the crowd and came towards us purposefully. I stared at her, hoping that it was not us she wanted, that she would turn in some other direction or go on past us. But she stopped.

She was a small, thin, gray-haired person, sharp-faced, with cold unwelcoming eyes. Her hair, under a shiny black straw hat, was knotted in a bun, and she wore a gray suit with a queer, long, double-breasted jacket, years out of date, and a skirt that came halfway down her calves. Her shoes were black and sensible, with laces. A gilt pin fastened her white silk blouse. Her lips were pressed tightly together and she frowned as she looked me up and down; I noticed that she had a mole on her chin from which three or four hairs sprouted.

"Mr. and Mrs. Strangeways?" she said. "Is this the little Frazer girl?"

My heart dropped into the pit of my stomach. Could this be my father's second wife? I could feel her hostility and disapproval towards me so much like an icy draft that instinctively I edged as far away from her as I could while she was talking to Mrs. Strangeways.

"Hm. Got enough luggage, haven't you," she said to me when the Strangeways had gone, taking with them, as it seemed, my only link with the world I had lost. "That means a taxi, I suppose. Lucky it isn't far."

The London streets were dark and wet: fallen leaves lay in pale drifts on the glistening pavements. I shivered with cold in my thin, pretty summer coat.

"Ridiculous," my companion sniffed, "sending you over in that outfit. Have to get you some decent sensible clothes, I suppose." She sounded aggrieved about it.

I hadn't heard the address she gave the driver, but pretty soon we stopped in a dark, quiet street of fairly big houses. There were trees with railings round them on the other side. It seemed quite unfamiliar. While I was still trying to believe that I really remembered it, I was roused by a brisk shake.

"Come on, child! You can't go to sleep in there! Hurry up and help with these things."

Dazedly, I helped carry my bags up a steep flight of front steps. The driver was paid off, grumbling at the smallness of his tip, and we went into a large, dimly lighted front hall.

A small man in a gray alpaca jacket appeared up some stairs from the basement, walking with a pronounced limp.

"You're soon back then, Milly," he remarked. "You got her, I see." He nodded sideways at me, but didn't look at or greet me.

"Soon back!" she sniffed. "I had to wait an age. The plane was three quarters of an hour late. Fog." She spoke as if it had been my fault.

"I'll take the bags up," he said, and limped off up another flight of stairs.

"*You*'d best go straight to bed," the woman called Milly said to me. "Do you want anything to eat?"

"No, thank you," I whispered. My throat ached and felt tight with tears.

"You'd better have some milk," she said. "I'll bring it presently. Go on up, now. It's the room on the right at the top of the second flight. You'll see where Arthur's put your things. Don't forget to wash. The bathroom's opposite."

Slowly, I climbed the steep stairs. By the time I found the room with my bags in it the man in the gray jacket had disappeared. *Could* he be my father? Surely not. If he were, surely I would have remembered him, found him familiar in some way. I pulled out a nightdress, washed skimpily, and scrambled into bed. After a while, the woman appeared with a glass of milk, surveyed my bags with a sour expression, said, "Have to get all those unpacked in the morning, I suppose," put out the light and went away, shutting the door.

The bed was cold, and I lay stiffly curled up, afraid to push my feet down into its icy depths. Having passed so much of the journey in sleep, I was now wide awake. I longed for more blankets or a hot water bottle but didn't dare get out of bed and go to ask for them.

By and by, I suppose I did fall into an uneasy slumber. And it was during that long, cold, troubled night that I had the dream for the first time—the terrifying, recurrent dream that was to come back and haunt me at intervals for the next ten years.

6

On that first occasion, I hadn't the least recollection, when I woke, as to what the dream had been about. I only knew that it had been unspeakably frightening. In fact, it wasn't until I'd been having it for several years that I began to remember dim fragments of it when I woke up. Each time it came back, which varied from periods of three to six months, seldom more, sometimes less—the familiar horror would grip me and *then*, in my sleep, I would remember and wait helplessly for it to take its usual course and lead to its awful climax. Between its visitations it faded from my mind like steam from a mirror, but then I would wake in the morning, rigid with terror, my heart banging, my mouth dry from a silent scream, knowing I'd had the dream again, but with nearly all traces of memory gone. That was a main part of its dreadfulness —the fact that it was always, so to speak, hidden behind a curtain in my mind. If I could have remembered it in daylight, analyzed it calmly and sensibly, I dare say it might not have been so bad. But the most I could ever recall of it, at that time, was that it was in some way connected with a *face*—a face that moved from one part of the darkness to another, a face that in some inexplicable, horrible way swung to and fro. . . . I grew to know that face as well as my own in the glass. I could have recognized it among thousands.

Children are secretive beings. I can see now that it was silly of me not to tell someone about it, but I was mortally ashamed of having the dream, certain that nobody else was troubled with such an affliction. It seemed like a sort of disease, almost like being mad or crippled. Not for worlds would I have talked about it—as far as possible I didn't even *think* about it. I used to hope, vaguely, that as I grew older it would get better, that when I reached that mysterious, sudden state

7

of being grown up, it would go away entirely, or that I'd be accustomed to it and indifferent to it.

Instead, it became worse and worse. The intervals between its assaults became wider, but the dream itself intensified and grew longer and more dreadful until. . . .

But I'm getting a long way ahead of myself, and away from the first time I had the dream, that bleak, wretched first night in London before I met George.

I woke up at five, trembling with cold and the aftermath of the dream—what I came later to call its aura, a sort of black unhappiness that often lasted right through the following day. It was impossible to get back to sleep, so I crept quietly out of bed and dressed. Presently, traffic started up in the street outside. A milkman's wagon jangled down the street and in due course stopped outside our house. As I peered out the window, the woman who had met me came out of the front door and called something, evidently a request for extra milk.

"Morning, missis! She came then, did she?" The milkman's face was alight with interest. "What's she like? Does she favor her mum?"

I couldn't hear Milly's reply but her shrug, as she took the bottles, gave evidence enough of her opinion.

Twenty minutes later, I was summoned down to breakfast. The other two members of the household seemed to have had theirs already; I choked down cornflakes alone in a cold gloomy dining room overlooking a small back garden. When I had finished, Milly helped me unpack my clothes and put them away.

"Haven't you any winter things at all?" she said disapprovingly.

"They were all too small . . . I've grown such a lot since last winter."

"Well, for school today you'd better wear this, it's about the warmest you've got. . . . Put it on quickly now, there's no time to lose and Arthur'll show you the way."

"School? Am I going to school?" I was apprehensive; I suppose I'd vaguely realized I'd be sent to school in England but hadn't expected it so soon.

"Well, I should hope so! Your father thought you'd best begin right away, better than moping about the house. So hurry up and change."

It seemed to me that she had spoken of Arthur and my father as if they were two different people, so, just as she was leaving the room, I summoned up courage to ask the question that had been in my mind for the last twelve hours:

"Where—where is my father?"

She said impatiently, as if she thought it quite unnecessary that I should be given the information, "He's away. In Edinburgh," and turned to go.

"When will he be back?"

"Not for another two weeks."

"Is he on holiday?"

"Oh, bother the child. No—he's at a doctors' conference in Edinburgh. That's all I know. Now stop asking questions, I've your school lunch to make."

"Is my father a doctor, then?"

She looked at me as if I were mentally deficient, opened her mouth, shut it again and finally said, "Yes. Don't be longer than five minutes, now."

I heard her steps go briskly down the stairs.

I CAN STILL REMEMBER ALMOST EVERY MINUTE OF THAT long first morning at school. I don't suppose I shall ever have an unhappier day. Most of the other girls didn't mean to be unfriendly I expect, but—after nearly four years' life in America—everything about me was queer, from my clothes to my accent. I heard tittered remarks wherever I went.

"Coo, Brenda! Dig the fancy shoes."

"Help. I'm fainting. Culottes!"

"Can I believe my eyes? Look at the sailor collar!"

My things seemed all right to me, but it was plain they were all wrong. And the lessons I had learned were different. I used the wrong words for things; I said grades instead of classes; I hadn't the right kind of pencils, or rulers, or equipment; I didn't understand the money; by the end of the morning I felt like a fool.

To make matters worse, the headmistress called me to her study just before lunch and told me kindly but firmly that she would prefer it if I didn't mention to the other girls that my mother had been quite a well-known movie actress.

"I didn't—I wouldn't—" was all I could stammer. The thought of *boasting* about Mother, at such a time, gave me a sick, horrified sensation.

"I'm sure you wouldn't now, my dear. The other teachers and I are all so sorry for your unhappy loss. But to avoid silly chatter among the other girls—and for your own sake too—I think it will be best if there is no talk about Hollywood and films and so on. Try to forget all that part of your life."

Forget Mother? The headmistress meant well, I'm sure, but her words seemed heartless, and the allusion to my loss brought tears which were still very near the surface. As we went into lunch, the girl called Brenda noticed and remarked loudly, "Boo hoo, what's up with little Miss Bermuda?"

I slunk to a corner and stooped over my sandwiches, trying to make myself invisible amid the roar of talk, laughter, and clatter that filled the big dining room.

At last, the horrible day dragged to an end. Limping Arthur appeared and surlily escorted me home, which caused more amusement to my classmates.

"Reckon you can find your own way from now on," he remarked as we walked slowly along, accommodating to his pace. When we reached the house, he said, "Your tea's laid out in the dining room," and limped off down the basement stairs.

I was longing for friendly company and had half a mind to follow him, though plainly I was not meant to. Hesitantly, I took two or three steps down the stairs and then stopped, as somewhere down below I heard my mother's name spoken.

". . . no better than she should be," the voice went on. "But what can you expect in the movies? They're all the same. Pity Mr. Edwin ever married her. And I shouldn't be a bit surprised if the young one takes after her. Same color hair—not a bit of Frazer in her. I'll bet she leads us a dance by and by, if there's not a firm hand kept on her. The *clothes* that child has got! More suitable for royalty than a schoolgirl her age. And not one decent warm thing among them. Little bits of frills—even a bikini! Disgusting, I call it."

A chair scraped, and I fled silently back up

the stairs to my lonely meal in the dining room. I was quite hungry by now—I couldn't eat my sandwiches at lunchtime—but the sight of the solitary plate of bread and butter, glass of milk and two ginger biscuits at one end of the long polished table depressed me unutterably. There was a french window in the room and openwork iron steps leading down to the garden. A yellow, watery sun had come out by now so, taking the plate and a cushion, I went out and sat on the steps. But I found I was still too miserable to eat. After a couple of bites, I shoved the plate on one side and put my head down on my knees. I couldn't help it—the loneliness of the day engulfed me, plus homesickness and bewilderment at the queer, unwelcoming atmosphere in this gloomy house. Although I tried to keep them back, tears ran down my cheeks, faster and faster.

And then, suddenly, I was aware of a soft, childish voice coming from somewhere up above me.

"George! George, look, there's somebody in the next door garden. D'you suppose she's. . . ."

A boy's voice said something cautionary in a lower tone, but the girl went on unchecked.

"She looks older than me—about the same age as you. Shall I call to her? D'you suppose she'll live here now? Well, I don't care what you say, I'm going to speak to her. She looks awfully miserable. *George*, she's crying!"

"Sh! Polly—wait! . . ."

But the warning was evidently unheeded, for I heard a scraping noise and looked up in time to see a small girl launch herself off the roof of a shed in the next door garden and land on my side of the fence. She seemed several years younger than I and was very pretty, with fair curls and large, appealing, blue eyes. She came running and plumped herself down close beside me on the steps, putting an arm round me confidingly.

"Are you lonely, poor thing? Cheer up, we'll keep you company. I'm Polly Barnard and that's my brother George up there on the roof. Is Dr. Frazer your father? I thought so. Have you come to live here now? Isn't London horrid? We haven't been here long—we used to live in Africa. What's your name? Meg? That's nice."

Her questions poured out so fast that I wasn't able to answer them all. I looked up at the shed and saw a boy of twelve or thirteen, fair-haired and blue-eyed like Polly. He nodded to me somewhat awkwardly.

"Come on, George!" called Polly. "She doesn't mind our being in her garden—do you? She's pleased to have company, aren't you? How old are you? I'm seven and George is twelve, we both go to day school but George is going to board soon. Do you think you'll like it here? We live with our aunt. Mummy and Daddy are still in Africa."

George came hesitantly toward us and gave me a cautious smile. He was wonderfully good-looking, quite the handsomest boy I had ever seen. He and Polly, with their sunny hair and blue eyes, were such a contrast to the depression of my day that I fell in love with both of them on the spot.

"I say," George said, looking round, "it's not very nice in this garden, is it? Not enough lawn. Why don't you come over into ours and we could play french cricket. Can you field?"

"I can field in baseball," I said doubtfully.

"Come on then."

"Yes, come on," echoed Polly, "and I'll show you my dolls' tea set."

I hesitated—but the tug of her friendly little

13

paw was hard to resist. Just at that moment, though, a disapproving voice from the window above called, "Miss Meg! Who are you talking to? Who's that in the garden?" and the limping Arthur appeared.

When he saw the children his face cleared, however, and he said:

"Oh, it's you two, is it? Thought it wouldn't be long before young Inquisitive was round. Over the fence, I suppose."

George looked abashed, but Polly, taking no notice, cried, "Can she come in our garden to play?"

"Don't see why not, but no climbing over the fence, mind. You go round by the front gate, decent, and come back before half-past six."

"Who is that man?" I asked in a low voice when we were safely in the Barnards' garden.

"Don't you *know*?" Polly was astonished. "He's Mr. Todd. He has very bad arthritis. That's why he limps. He's married to Mrs. Todd, who's your father's housekeeper."

"*Oh*." I drew a long breath. A load was lifted from my mind. "I see. I thought perhaps she was my father's wife."

"No, Dr. Frazer isn't married any more now. Goodness, fancy not knowing a thing like that about your own father! How funny." George scowled at Polly reprovingly, but she chattered on disregarding him, tucking her arm through mine. "An old aunt of your father's used to live in that house. She died two or three years ago and left him the house, and Mr. and Mrs. Todd used to look after the aunt, so now they look after your father. He's quite nice—just think, I know him better than you do! He's tired-looking and rather quiet, but he's kind—when I cut my leg he bandaged it up and gave me an injection and he said

14

I was a Trojan. No, I mean a Spartan. Your mother died, didn't she? Poor Meg. Never mind, you can come and play with us whenever you like. Aunt Hilda isn't as nice as Mummy but she isn't bad, she won't mind."

Polly never stopped talking. Moreover, she had and still has the most amazing knack of extracting information from people. The milkman, the postman, her Aunt Hilda, the policeman on the beat, even the surly Mr. Todd, all succumbed to her charm and let drop more information than they intended. The upshot of this was that Polly was able to tell me far more about my father than I knew myself.

"He's a doctor, and he went to help in the Korean War because he knows a lot about foreign diseases. And he was taken prisoner, and put in a camp, and then he got ill himself. And by the time he came back, your mother had fallen in love with someone else, and she went off and married him and your father divorced her."

"Other way 'round, nitwit," George put in loftily. "He divorced her and *then* she married again. Otherwise it would have been bigamy."

"What does it matter which way 'round? Was he nice, the other husband she married?"

"Yes, very," I said sadly.

"Well, your father's not bad. He still wasn't well when your mother left him, so he came and lived with his aunt, old Miss Frazer next door, and Mr. and Mrs. Todd looked after him till he was better. So they are very fond of him, *jealously devoted*, Aunt Hilda says. They thought it was pretty mean of your mother to go off and leave him."

"Well, she couldn't help it if she fell in love with Ralph," I defended her. "And it wasn't her fault he fell ill."

15

"No, perhaps not," Polly agreed fairly. "And Mr. Todd said she was very fond of parties. And I think your father never would take her to any, so that can't have been very nice for her."

Did that ring a bell? Mother at the mirror, in a filmy dress, pinning a flower into her coppery hair —"Do come too, Edwin, ducky, I'm sure it would do you good to get out and about." "My dear, I should loathe it. You know I bore your theater friends and they bore me."

"Your mother used to act in plays in London before she went to Hollywood, didn't she?" Polly said, dovetailing into my thought.

"I've seen pictures of her in old magazines," George remarked. "You're not very like her, are you? Too skinny. But your hair's the same color."

I thought of Mrs. Todd's remarks about coloring and stage people.

"It's because I'm like Mother that Mrs. Todd doesn't like me," I said slowly. "Because Mother left him."

"Never mind," Polly consoled. "If she's horrid to you, you can always come round here." She gave me a little pat.

"Come on," said George. "It'll be too dark to play cricket soon."

Such was the beginning of my long alliance with the two Barnards. Of course, nobody could help loving Polly. And Polly had such an unquestioning, hero-worshiping adoration for George that I naturally followed her example. Together, we followed him about, fetched and carried for him, held the bait and basket while he fished in the Serpentine, fielded while he batted, trotted after with the ball of string when he flew his kite, and watched admiringly from a stipulated distance while he ran his electric trains, which females

16

were strictly forbidden to touch. And in return, he did our sums, sharpened our pencils, taught us to swim and skate and, later, to jive, twist, and shake.

But I'm getting ahead again.

On the day Father was due home from his conference (Polly had found out the date, I'm sure Mrs. Todd would never have told me), I hurried home from school feeling quite weak with anxiety and anticipation.

School wasn't so bad now. Mrs. Todd had bought me clothes—hideous, but exactly like those of the other girls which was all that mattered—I had learned my way about and managed to sink into the crowd. I was accepted. Some classes—dancing, and drawing, and languages—I even enjoyed.

But life at home was as bleak as ever. Three times a day I was given my meals alone in the gloom of the chilly dining room. When I asked, humbly, if I couldn't eat with Mr. and Mrs. Todd, comfortably in the kitchen, Mrs. Todd drew herself up prim-lipped and said that Frazer would never have allowed such a thing.

So I continued to eat on my own. Otherwise, I was expected to help with housework to the extent of dusting, polishing, running errands, and keeping my own room clean, which I enjoyed. At least I felt useful. I hoped that, in time, Mrs. Todd's hostility would die down.

But all the time I longed for and feared my father's arrival. How would he feel towards me? Was he lonely? Would he be pleased to have me living with him? It seemed odd that he hadn't had time to write from Scotland, not even a post card, but Polly said that the medical conference he had been attending was an important one, and that he'd made several speeches on tropical medicine.

When I entered our street on that cold, dry,

autumn day I saw an unfamiliar car parked before our steps. As soon as I ran into the house, Mrs. Todd shot out of the study like a spider, shutting the door behind her.

"Hush!" she whispered. "I've told you time and *again* not to bang the door. You might think of others —specially when the master's just home and tired out. I've put your tea in your room. You go up there now and stay up there."

"Can't I see him?" I was dreadfully dashed.

"Not now, he's resting. Go on, hop it." She nodded fiercely toward the stairs before retreating backward through the doorway.

I loitered on the way up, hoping that a voice from the study would countermand her order and call me down. Instead, listening with all my ears, I heard a man's voice say, "Is that the child?" and Mrs. Todd answer something in a low voice. He replied in a tone of weary indifference, "Not now. Later, perhaps."

Bitterly cast down, I crept on up the stairs to my own bedroom where, curled up on the window seat, I ate my tea and did my homework.

Presently, looking down, I saw Mrs. Todd set off up the road, a shopping basket on her arm, a purposeful expression on her face; laying in extra delicacies for "the master" no doubt.

It seemed a good moment to slip out. I tiptoed downstairs. The study door was ajar. The table lamp glowed and the fire flickered. Dusk filled the room.

My father was sitting in an armchair by the fire, sorting through a large pile of letters. I recognized him at once. He was gray-faced and gray-haired, just as I remembered him. He didn't hear me come in, being absorbed in a letter.

I cleared my throat and said, "Hello, Father. It's me."

He looked up at that, frowning, resting the sheet of paper on his knee.

"Didn't I hear Mrs. Todd tell you to go up and do your homework?" he said.

"Yes, she did. But I've done it—mostly. I wanted to come and—and—"

"I must make it quite clear right away that children aren't ever allowed in this room," he said. "When I'm in here, I'm working and not to be bothered. Understand?"

"Yes," I whispered.

"Very well. And you must do what Mrs. Todd says. She tells me you are sometimes rather rude and sulky. She does a great deal for us, and she's not used to having a child in the house, making extra work and cooking, so you must help her, not hinder."

"I do help her," I muttered, but he went on unheeding.

"Now, I'm very busy catching up with all the letters that have come while I was away, so run along like a good child. I'll talk to you later; tomorrow, perhaps."

I was retreating, my throat tight with tears of mortification, when he said suddenly, "Wait. . . ."

He pulled a string beside him, switching on an overhead light, and studied me for a moment or two. I bit my lip, staring at the ground. I heard him sigh.

"Are you sorry I've come to live here?" I was astonished to hear myself ask.

He sounded surprised. "Sorry? What a silly thing to say. This is your home, of course. Where else could you live? Run along now. Shut the door after you, please."

I heard the click as he switched off the light again, a second before the door closed.

Drawing a long, shaky breath, I went into the

dining room next door and stood there, absently tracing a pattern on the polished mahogany table with my finger. I noticed the table was already laid for dinner: one place, with silver, and a glass, and a fine, white, damask table napkin.

Suddenly, there came a tap at the french window and two eager faces were pressed close to it, pink and shining against the dusk beyond.

"Psst! Meg! Here! Psst!"

I flew across the room and opened the window.

"Well? Has he come?"

I slipped out to them, closing the window behind me, and Polly gripped my arms impatiently, fairly jumping up and down in her curiosity.

"Well? Did you like him? Was he pleased to see you? Was he the way you remembered him? D'you think he's nice?"

"I don't know. . . ."

My voice must have sounded depressed, for Polly instantly abandoned her usual flow of questions and said comfortably:

"Oh, well. P'raps he's tired. Anyway, what we came 'round to tell you was, Aunt Hilda says we can have a bonfire and sparklers in our garden, and roast chestnuts and potatoes, and can you come?"

"You can have half my sparklers," George said generously.

"All right," I said, overjoyed. "Just let me get my coat!"

I was never so glad to go with them. . . .

BUT THE FOLLOWING WEEK HODGE ARRIVED, AND THAT made a tremendous difference in my life. I'd been wondering vaguely, off and on, about my Aunt Venetia, Mother's elder sister, now my only relative on Mother's side. As far as I could recall from when I'd last seen her, five or six years back, she was utterly different from Mother, being small, brisk, and dumpy, but nice.

Now, since Father seemed so uninterested in me, and the Todds verging on downright hostility, I began to brood about whether it wouldn't be possible for me to go and live with Aunt Venetia. Only where *did* she live? I referred to Polly who, for a wonder, didn't know; she suggested hunting in the London telephone directory, but Venetia wasn't listed there. While I was screwing my courage to the point of asking my father if he knew her address, two letters arrived from her simultaneously. One, forwarded from California, had followed me slowly across the Atlantic; the other, much more recent, was addressed to me care of my father in London. Both bore Lebanese stamps. The earlier one, which must have missed me by a couple of days, simply said:

> Dear Meg, Ask someone to cable for me if you need me. You must be very unhappy but I'm sure you are being brave about it. Love and sympathy, Venetia.

Later I came to realize how characteristic that note was, combining warm-heartedness and thrift—

21

Venetia would never send a cable where a letter would do or use three sentences if she could express her meaning in two, but her feelings were nonetheless real for being concisely expressed.

The second letter—I now noticed that both were headed Beirut University—said:

Dear Meg, I'm glad to hear that, as I expected, you are going to live with your father. That will be best for both of you, and you'll get a good education in London. My quarters out here aren't very suitable for having you with me, but my appointment lasts only four years, so when I come back to London we'll arrange to see plenty of each other. Meantime, as you may feel a little strange at first, I'm organizing some companionship for you via Harrods Pet Department. Love, Venetia.

My heart sank a little. Four years, just then, seemed an endless time to wait. But the last sentence stirred my curiosity. I didn't have long to wait before the promised companionship arrived in a hamper. And it was Hodge. At that time he was about the size of a blackboard eraser, hedgehog-colored, golden-eyed, with a vaguely marked black stripe running from ears to tail along his back.

"What's *that*, for goodness' sake?" sniffed Mrs. Todd. "Some kind of a *cat?* I shouldn't think for a moment Dr. Frazer will allow it to stay in the house," and I was in dread that she had prophesied truly, for already I'd lost my heart to Hodge, who had instantly burrowed his sandy nose inside my arm, against my ribs, and was purring like a power mower. But—again characteristically—Venetia had made a shrewd choice. She didn't care for cats herself because they gave her asthma, but she knew that Father liked them.

"Nonsense. Children ought to have pets," he

said briskly, in answer to Mrs. Todd's jeremiads and mutterings. "It will be good for Meg to learn to look after it. Besides, an Abyssinian's not like an ordinary cat—much more sensible and affectionate. And it won't need to be taken for walks as a dog would. It was a good idea of Miss Venetia's."

To my surprise, I discovered that Father entertained the greatest respect for Venetia, perhaps because of her total difference from Mother. She had, I learned, a degree in sociology and lectured on this subject to the Lebanese.

Hodge became at once the focal point of my life. As soon as I got home from school, he would rush out to greet me, arching his muscular back, sticking his tail up like a flag of welcome, purring louder than a helicopter. He was ready to play wild games every minute of the day, and his tight-curled presence in the crook of my knees made all the difference at night when I woke strangling with terror after a visitation by the dream; to disperse the memory of that unknown, dreaded face on its awful pendulum swing through the dark, I could reach down and feel for his round furry head; he was never too sleepy to respond with a short snatch of purr.

So things gradually grew better. I was not so unhappy again as in those first few weeks.

It took ages for Father to accept me; in a way, he never has. If ever I kissed him, or gave him a birthday present, or asked him to do something special for me, such as coming to see me act in a school play, a sort of shutter would close down over him, and I would feel him retreat, warily, from too great an intimacy. In the end, I learned that it was better not to risk the rebuffs that I invariably received. But we went for walks in the park together sometimes, and to concerts and art exhibitions, which we both enjoyed. We had a stock of mild little jokes at mealtimes about simple, superficial things, the weather and the food, funny news items, outings, and the few books we enjoyed in common. Father liked Polly and George, approved of them, and encouraged our friendship—for one thing, it got me out of the house. He was also cautiously pleased with my progress at school. And he really loved Hodge, who was much more of a link between us than our father-daughter relationship. Rather absurdly, we always found it easier to talk to one another when Hodge was in the room.

Best of all, when I had been there three years, Mr. Todd's arthritis got so bad that he and his wife had to retire to Worthing. Father found a new housekeeper, a kind, plump, unexacting widow called Mrs. Stoker, and she and I liked each other from the first. Now, I thought hopefully, everything would be all right.

But it didn't really work out that way. My dream began to come oftener, and worse. Sometimes, during the black aura of depression that followed it, I wondered if Father *knew* that I had it—though I didn't see how he could—and if that was why he avoided a close relationship with me, because he found me queer, abnormal, tainted in some way.

Unfortunately, just at this time, I lost sight of both Polly and George. Polly was packed off to finishing school in Paris, George had gone into the Guards. I was seventeen now, crazy about painting. While I painted or drew I could forget my dream, my loneliness, my unsatisfactory relationship with Father, everything. The art teacher at school was helpful and enthusiastic. But when I asked Father if I could go to an art school in Paris, so as to be near Polly, he utterly refused. I could get no explanation out of him, just the flat negative.

I was bitterly hurt and disappointed.

"But, Father, *why* not? I won't do anything silly. I'm awfully sensible, really I am! I could board at Polly's school and go to classes every day, she says lots of people do. Please let me! What's your reason for not?"

"I would prefer not to discuss it, Meg."

To do him justice, he immediately arranged for me to begin at a London art school, but this couldn't completely heal the breach caused by his lack of confidence in me.

Trying to distract my mind from the unhappy tension at home, I threw myself into my studies and worked like mad. Portraits, in particular, were beginning to fascinate me. I've always had a queer interest in faces—even when I was very small and used to get scolded for staring; I'm endlessly fascinated by the variations of eye and nose, neck and jaw; what makes one set of features different from another. I can see now that this interest was really connected with my dream, but at first I didn't realize that. Fairly soon the principal of the art school began to take a good deal of interest in me and be encouraging; he had several talks with Father, who came out of his reports on bilharzia long enough to agree to my taking up portrait painting as a career. And—this I kept from Father at first because the chances of my winning seemed so unlikely—the principal also suggested that I should work for a three-year scholarship, offered by the trustees of the school, which would if I won supply enough money for me to go and study in Paris.

I had begun to wonder if Father's refusal to let me go abroad was really because we were hard up; he would never talk about finance, but it was the only explanation that seemed reasonable. He wasn't very well

25

and talked of retiring soon; since the Todds had left, a good many rooms in our house were closed, and we lived very quietly. Anyway, I thought, if I won the scholarship, Father's objections to my going to Paris *must* be removed.

Round about this time Venetia moved back to London. Her Beirut appointment had been extended, and then extended again—the Lebanese knew when they were on to a good thing, apparently—but she finally declared that she was fed up with the climate and pined for a nice, damp English summer. She came home, took a lectureship at London University and found a house in Holland Park which she shared with two friends. Her presence was a huge comfort. We'd always corresponded regularly, but her letters were brief and confined to practical matters.

Now that she was settled in London, I saw her almost every day, for she made over her big downstairs room for me as a studio. It was marvelous to have someone who would talk about Mother; Venetia, I soon gathered, had often been exasperated and sometimes dismayed by the behavior of her younger sister but had loved her dearly nonetheless.

"Was she really a good actress?" I asked once. I was sketching Venetia and so had her captive, sitting in a characteristic position, feet up on a hassock, her portable typewriter propped on her short, sturdy legs, and her head tilted sideways to avoid the smoke of a cigarette in the corner of her mouth.

"Fizz was a *marvelous* actress," Venetia answered crossly. "I haven't any time for the theater—never had—and it was the wrong profession for her. Saw too many of the wrong kinds of people. But she could get inside the skin of a part better than anyone I've ever seen since. She had that kind of sensitivity. You've got it too. It's not an advantage."

"Ralph wasn't the wrong kind of person for her," I objected. "He loved her, and he was terribly kind."

Venetia sighed. "Maybe. Of course Fizz should *never* have married your father. She and Edwin were both far too young at the time anyway. The whole thing was a dreadful pity—except from my point of view, because now I have a beautiful niece to make me tea when I come home hoarse from lecturing."

Her face lit up with its rare smile. Venetia is not demonstrative but she is a darling. You feel her warmth and integrity as soon as you meet her. I had even briefly considered telling her about my dream. If I could ever bring myself to talk about it to anybody, Venetia would be the obvious person; her mixture of kindness and common sense might, conceivably, reduce the problem to bearable proportions. But it was no use; after keeping it to myself for so long, I just *couldn't* force myself to bring it out into the daylight.

That was before the Paris business.

Naturally, it was to Venetia that I rushed when the fantastic, unbelievable news came that I had won the Paris scholarship—not only that, but had sold two of the portraits I submitted, "Venetia at Typewriter" and another, for a sum that would last me at least six months with careful living.

Venetia was just as delighted as I, but to my dismay she was equally worried about Father's reactions. She agreed to come round then and there to break the news to him and point out its advantages and economies.

We had a miserable scene—as I'd half expected. Venetia was reasonable and calm, but I became more and more frantic.

Father simply said that I was too young to go to Paris on my own.

"But Edwin, she's nearly nineteen now," Venetia

pointed out. "Lots of girls have jobs and are leading independent lives at that age. Some are even married." I could see *that* was the wrong thing to say; Father's face shut like a trap. But Venetia went on:

"Meg can support herself by her own work, she's proved it with these portraits. She needn't be an expense to you. And you can't deny that she's worked hard for this scholarship."

"It may all be a flash in the pan," Father said flatly. "And even if it isn't—even if she does have real talent," he sounded thoroughly skeptical, "I still say she hasn't the stability to live in Paris on her own. She's too like. . . ." He bit off his words uncomfortably.

I jumped up, hurt and resentful. "*That*'s what it is!" I burst out. "You hate me because I'm like Mother, isn't that it? You grudge my success because *she* was successful! Oh, it's unfair! What do you know about me, anyway? We're practically strangers to one another!"

"It's because I remember what success did to her."

"How do you know what *I'm* like?"

"Meg, dear," Venetia said, "wait, don't. . . ."

But I didn't wait. I stormed out of the room, out of the house. Father's injustice made me feel physically weak and shaken. Why should the fact that Mother had left Father fourteen years before be visited on *me, now?*

Half blind with tears I started down the street, going nowhere in particular. Almost at once, I ran slap up against somebody. A man's voice said:

"I say, I'm most terribly sorry. Did I hurt you? I didn't mean. . . . Why, good lord—it's *Meg!*"

I stepped back, blinking away tears, and looked up. His arm still supported me. It was a man with a mustache—no—good heavens—it was *George*, tall, tanned, decisive-looking, bigger in every way than I remembered him. He was staring at me, almost gaping.

I said shakily, trying to laugh:

"George! Where did you spring from?"

He still looked dazed. He said, "I've just come home. Decided to leave the army, buy a bowler and set up in the City. Didn't I write to you about it?"

"No, you didn't. You're a hopeless letter writer, George."

"Well," he admitted, "there never seems to be time for letters. But I say, Meg, you have cha—— You are pretty now! I'd hardly have believed it! Scrawny little thing you used to be."

"Thanks," I said vaguely, still too shaken by the recent scene to be cheered by compliments.

"No, I mean it." George studied me with earnest attention. "You're so like the pictures of your mother. I say, Meg, though, are you all right? You look a bit seedy, matter of fact—you were rushing along the street at a devil of a lick."

"Father won't let me go and study art in Paris, and I flew off the handle a bit."

"The old skinflint!" George said. "I expect he thinks it would be a waste of money, mind you—he'd pay your fees, and then some gay blade of an art student would up and marry you. Tell you what—*I'll* take you to Paris. And Poll could come along too, it'd be quite respectable. I'll talk your father 'round, don't worry."

I could see he hadn't quite got the idea.

"But I want to live there and work, George."

"Oh well, you might change your mind once you saw the place. There's nowhere like London really. Anyway, relax, I bet I can fix it. I always could get 'round your dad better than you could, remember? Are you doing anything this evening? No? Marvelous! Why don't you come out and have a bite with me, and we'll go somewhere we can dance and discuss a plan of campaign?"

"All right," I said. It was wonderfully comforting to have George taking charge of me.

I ran back to our house. Venetia had gone, feeling, I suppose, that she couldn't mend matters by staying. But Father looked as if she'd spoken her mind to him pretty freely; he seemed subdued, almost remorseful. Hodge was sitting on his lap, paws tucked, eyes closed. The one consoling element in the Paris disappointment, I suddenly thought, was that I wouldn't have to leave Hodge.

"George is back," I said coldly. "I'm going out with him."

"George? George who? One of your art students?" Father was instantly suspicious again.

"No, *George*—from next door."

"Oh, *George*—" An expression of relief crossed his face. "*He*'s back, is he? You'll be all right with him. Have a good time then—my dear." he added awkwardly. Hodge turned his head, shifting his dispassionate, slit-eyed gaze from Father to me.

It was a consoling evening. George couldn't get over the improvement in my looks—he kept coming back to it. And—which I found even more sustaining—he seemed highly impressed by the story of my scholarship and the two pictures sold.

"Clever little thing you turned out to be!" he said several times in a tone of wonder, as if some dusty unconsidered ornament on the mantelpiece had unexpectedly been identified as a rare bit of Sèvres. Used to years of being despised by George as a no-account female appendage, I found this new admiration as good as a warm bath after Father's disapproval. George had always seemed almost like a relation, and there's nothing nicer than having one's dazzling talents suddenly discovered by members of one's hitherto unappreciative family.

So we were delighted with one another. After dinner, he drove me out to Newlands Corner in his Citroën, passing everything on the way; he seemed so confident that I wasn't even frightened when we took curves at seventy on the wrong side of the road. We looked at the stars, large as snowcones in the sky, and then George kissed me. I burst out crying.

"What's the matter?" he said, rather startled—evidently this was not a response he had encountered often. "Didn't you like it?"

"Oh, yes—yes, I did. . . ." How could I possibly begin to explain the complicated tangle of emotions which his embrace had fetched up to the surface? Particularly, how could I explain it to plain, straightforward George; he wouldn't understand what the devil I was going on about.

"*Well*, then . . ." and he took me in a firmer grip, breaking off once to remark, "honestly, I can't get over the luck of finding you like this!"

It seemed the most unparalleled stroke of luck to me, too; we drove back to London like two prospectors who have uncovered a twenty-four carat vein. And two weeks later, we announced our engagement.

George wanted to get married as soon as possible, but my father disapproved of that—his own disastrous early marriage loomed large among his objections—and for once, I was on his side.

"Blast him!" George grumbled, with the tiniest edge on his normal good nature. "*I'm* certain enough now! Darling, beautiful Meg, I want to have you all to myself—and then I want to dress you up in mink and emeralds"—George had got off to a good start in the City, I gathered, thanks to a lot of well-placed uncles— "and take you to the Caprice every night to show off to everyone what a prize I've got!"

"George, you are sweet!"

I couldn't get over the happiness of being loved and valued—George's face every time we met was like Christmas, and bank holidays, and birthdays all rolled into one. It no longer mattered that Father had been so unreasonable about Paris. Anyway, George had promised that we should live there for a year after we were married. And, meanwhile, I was having such a good time that the postponement of Paris didn't worry me. For the principal of my art school, sympathizing with my disappointment over the scholarship, had got me a couple of portrait commissions, which quickly led to others. My work suddenly caught on. In a mild way I even became quite well known. I'd painted a tubby little Sheikh (business contact of George's) and a shy, young, Scandinavian royal debutante (who'd been to Polly's expensive finishing school), there was a piece about me in a glossy weekly, a headline in a flighty daily, and overnight, I found myself launched, to my astonishment, as a society painter.

Of course, half of it was Polly's doing. She floated back from her French finishing school, found her feet in London at once, and proceeded to whisk me after her through all the upper crust circles in which she seemed so thoroughly at home.

I became used to hearing her say airily in her soft little voice, "This is our friend, Meg Frazer. You know, *the* Meg Frazer; everyone's having their portrait done by her. . . ."

Life suddenly became fun. And work flooded in.

I had to start turning down commissions. I was booked up for months ahead. When I went to sleep at night, endless faces danced before my closed lids—young, smooth faces, old, successful faces, elegant, enameled faces, gnarled faces full of character—sometimes, I could hardly sleep.

That was one cause of the trouble.

Father didn't like my success, either; not at all. In fact, he actually volunteered the suggestion that it might be a good thing, after all, if we got married in the summer, instead of waiting till the autumn as originally planned. And George was all for this, too. But where eight or nine months ago I'd have agreed like a shot, now I was oddly reluctant, oddly uncertain. Perhaps it was just that I didn't want to lose my lovely sparkling freedom too soon.

George and Father weren't pleased. And that was another part of the trouble.

The worst part of all I kept to myself: which, of course, was my dream. When we first got engaged, t had stopped entirely for three months, but now it seemed to be making up for lost time. And I didn't want to tell George about it. I couldn't imagine that he'd be helpful; he loathed illness or eccentricity because it scared him. On the other hand, something would have to be done before we were married, or some night I'd be giving him the shock of his life, when I woke, beside myself with terror.

But I postponed making a decision, and kept on postponing it.

So, good and bad, gay and busy and complicated, my nineteenth summer drew toward its close, until one evening, strolling with George on the Embankment, I happened to say:

"If we're getting married early in October, I suppose we ought to start thinking about Paris apartments, shouldn't we?"

"Paris?" said George blankly.

I gave his arm a little impatient shake. "Wake up, honey! A flat in Paris for us when we're married. I must fix up about art classes, too."

George looked thunderstruck. "You're not serious? Live in Paris *now*? Just when work's going so well?" He went on to prove, with facts and figures, why it would be quite impossible to leave London for more than a few weeks during the next three years.

"But—you promised!" I said limply.

"Rubbish, darling. Live in Paris? You must be crazy. Of course, we'll stay there for our honeymoon, and for a weekend from time to time. But as for *living* there —that's quite out of the question. After all, you've got your bits and pieces of portraits over here to keep you busy. And you won't have so much time for painting once we're married."

I gave up arguing fairly soon. What was the point? I could see that George was really convinced he had never made a promise. And I felt a bit dazed; the situation called for some readjustments. It hadn't been the loss of Paris for the second time that shook me so much as the discovery that my future husband possessed such a thorough-going capacity for forgetting promises that proved awkward to keep. I would have preferred it if he'd said, "Look, darling, it's an awful nuisance, but it really wouldn't be convenient for me to live in Paris just now. I made that promise in a moment of rash enthusiasm, and I'm very sorry for your disappointment."

Something like that. It would have been more honest anyway.

At this point, it occurred to me that George didn't

seem very concerned about my pursuit of art. "Bits and pieces of portraits" indeed! His enthusiasm for me as a collector's piece, an all-around working model, talented as well as pretty, was insensibly being modified; or rather, *I* was to be modified into something more utilitarian.

"George," I said suddenly, pausing, "shall you expect me to do a lot of entertaining when we're married?"

"Entertaining?" He looked at me, puzzled. "Why, of course! Half the secret of a good business career lies with the executive's wife. Why?"

"Oh—nothing. I just wondered."

"Don't worry, love. You'll pass all the tests with flying colors. All the old directors will be falling over themselves to get asked to our dinners."

"George, I'm feeling a bit tired. I think I'll get on a bus and go home."

"I'll find a taxi," said George, and did. He would win first prize in any taxi-catching contest. "Yes, you do look a bit peaked," he added solicitously. "Take it easy, now. You ought to cut down on all this painting, you know."

So I went home, and I went to bed, but I didn't get a good sleep. . . .

I WOKE SCREAMING THAT TIME. IT TOOK ABOUT TEN minutes before I was really back into my body again— before I was me, myself, Meg Frazer, in a muck sweat, ice cold and trembling in my big comfortable bed. The dream's terror slowly receded, uncurling its grip on me tendril by tendril, leaving only its aftermath, like the acrid smell after a fire—vague memory of pain and falling; sharp, particular memory of the face.

"This can't be borne," somebody stammered in a hoarse, shaky voice. Presently, I understood that it was my own voice. Oddly, this steadied me, because I realized that what it said was true. Such a state of affairs could go on no longer. Something had to be done.

I stretched and sat up, aware now of the tension slowly unlocking from my cramped muscles and the traces of recent tears in my eyes and throat. By far the worst part was the barrier of waking; I felt as if another Meg had lain sleeping in my bed, convulsed with terror and anguish, struggling to wake, and I could not reach through to help her until she fought her own way to daylight.

A cold shower helped me pull myself together. At least, it washed away the traces of that other Meg's tears.

Hodge, who had left my bed for the patch of early sunshine on the window sill, unrolled his short gold-brown length, stretched till his muscles knotted, and strolled over with tail at masthead position to rub against my ankles.

I curled up on the window seat, for it was still very early, hours to breakfast, and looked out into the street, watching the milkman work his way along, remembering my first morning in that house. Superficially, this one was different enough: a fine September day. The grass in the square was heavy with dew, and the dahlias were blazing. I told myself that the dream had been brought back by prewedding nerves; any doctor would say that was what ailed me: prewedding nerves.

Hodge settled down for another snooze on my lap. He was ten, now, after all, with the sedate habits of middle age. Except when he forgot himself and behaved like a two-year-old.

Nerves. A doctor would say that all I needed was a tranquilizer. But of course I didn't intend to go to a *doctor;* I'd never hear the last of it from George if I did. Wasn't there a doctor in the family, anyway? And if *he* didn't notice anything wrong. . . .

By the time I finally went down, Father had already finished his breakfast and was deep in the *British Medical Journal.* He failed to notice my lack of appetite. His little weekend bag, packed, sat by the door, and I remembered with a slight sinking of the heart that he was going off to yet another of his medical conferences, leaving me alone in the house. Mrs. Stoker no longer lived in, since her married daughter had moved to a house not far away.

"Where is it this time—Bristol?"

"Liverpool." He looked at me absently over the top of the *B.M.J.* "Well—I'll see you on the thirtieth," he added, rustling his correspondence together and standing up, his mind already more than half elsewhere.

"Don't forget I'm getting married on the sixth."

"My dear Meg, I'm hardly likely to forget that, I hope." There was a clear note of relief in Father's tones. He added conscientiously, "Shall you be seeing George today?"

I nodded. "Yes, this evening. And lunch. He's picking Polly and me up at the studio."

"My regards to him," Father said. I thought— with a wry interior grin—that Father's approval of George was amply demonstrated by his lack of hesitation in going off and leaving me alone in the house. Some boy friends would take advantage of such a situation, but not George. Not reliable, conventional, well-conducted George.

After drinking three cups of black coffee, I walked across the park to Venetia's house. Hodge wanted to come, too. "You *know* you give her asthma," I told him, shutting him in, and he gave me a reproachful yellow glare.

Venetia was in her garden, weeding. She took one look at me and said:

"Meg, *darling*. What the *devil* have you been up to?"

"I'm all right," I said. "Honestly."

"Your looks don't flatter you then. Shall I ring Polly and tell her not to come?"

"No, I feel like painting. Besides, here she is."

A taxi had stopped by the gate and Polly floated out of it like a bit of thistledown looking silly but sweet in sugar pink.

She wandered into the studio and settled on the model's throne; I went on with the portrait which was going to be bride's gift to groom. George was still very fond of his little sister whom he treated as if the gap between their ages were fifteen years instead of five.

Venetia looked at me in a worried way and then went off shopping, but announced that she would be back after lunch and that she wanted to have a talk with me.

"P'raps she's going to tell you the facts of life," Polly said giggling.

"Keep still, you moved," I told her austerely, but she gave me an unrepentant grin. Her silliness was comforting. "Is the thought of matrimony beginning to get you down?" she said suddenly. "It would *me*. Specially to George." Polly's hero worship had worn thinner as she grew up. "He's bringing a list of presents people want to give you, by the way. Aunt Emma's is a plated biscuit barrel. You could keep jewelry in it. Or Hodge's cat biscuits. You're going to have a bit of trouble over Hodge when you're married, incidentally. George isn't really keen on cats. He wants a St. Bernard."

"We'll have to sort it out somehow," I said. I

had enough problems; I couldn't begin worrying over that one now.

Then George arrived in the Citroën, hot from the stock market. He kissed me and told Polly she'd got paint on her nose and looked like a guttersnipe. This was his way of advising me that *I*'d better tidy up; he hated criticizing me directly. Polly pouted and cooed while I did a quick change and George looked at his watch.

We had rather a harassed lunch. Apparently, the bears had got the bulls cornered, or it may have been the other way 'round, and George had to get back into the arena as soon as possible. He did, however, just remember to pull out a little box and hand it to me.

"Ring," he said.

He hadn't given me a ring when we first got engaged because his father had an insurance policy that was due to ripen (or whatever they do) in eight months' time. Since we had to wait a year to marry, he said, we might as well wait and get a decent ring, too. So in the meantime, I'd been wearing a dear little ring of his grandmother's, opal and pearls.

I opened the box. Inside was a slender band with what looked like a chunk of oxheart attached to it.

"You did say you liked rubies, didn't you?" George said. I felt affectionate toward him because, for once in his life, he had made a mistake.

"Well—actually—I thought topaz. Or garnet."

"Rubies are better," pronounced George.

"Not with my hair," I mentioned mildly, and Polly cried, "Sweetie, she can't possibly wear that! Not a gingerknob like Meg!"

George glanced at his watch in a hunted manner, and I hastily said, "Of course it's *lovely*—anyway never mind now. . . ." and he paid the bill and found us a taxi.

"See you tonight," he said. We were all going to the show at the Collodeon. "I'll pick you up at seven sharp."

So, WHAT WITH ONE THING AND ANOTHER, I WAS NOT feeling any more relaxed when I got back to Venetia's. She had made a jug of iced tea and was stretched out in a chair under her little plane tree when I joined her.

She put down the report on Kinship Groups she was reading and gave me a sharp look.

"Come on—out with it. Are you beginning to think you're making a mistake in marrying George?"

"Oh, no," I said. I couldn't afford to think anything of that kind. Arrangements were too far advanced. "No, it isn't anything to do with George, really. . . . It's just this rotten dream I keep having."

There was a long silence. Venetia looked at me, waiting. She has an amazing force of personality; on occasions like this, you really feel it. Even so, getting started was like trying to haul out the Sea Serpent with a six-penny fishing rod.

At last, I took a huge breath and said:

"I expect it'll sound stupid when it's put into words."

I poured myself a glass of tea. Venetia waited.

"It's a dream I've been having for years—ever since I was little. Mostly it comes every two or three months—but just lately it's been more like once a week, and it's no joke——"

"Prewedding strain making it worse," Venetia said. "But what's the dream about?"

"Well, nothing very much. The usual kind of

40

nightmare. First I'm on a steep place and falling—the ground's slipping away beneath me, and I'm trying to struggle across a strip of loose, shaly stuff, and I *know* that in the end I shall overbalance and fall down a long way and hurt myself badly."

"Insecurity," Venetia said, sliding a page of her report back into its folder. "Broken family. Mother died when you were only nine. It's all quite straightforward."

"Still, that doesn't explain the end of the dream."

"There's more?"

"Yes, the worst part. After I fall over the cliff—which I can *feel*, all the way from top to bottom—it all gets much more frightening. I'm in horrid pain, then, and I'm put somewhere that's all shut in and dark except for one dim little light. I know something terrible is going to happen. It's connected with a face, a face that I can see coming towards me out of the dark. And then . . . then it happens."

"What happens?"

"I don't know. I can never remember."

"Talking to a psychiatrist might help," Venetia suggested doubtfully.

"And have George think I was going out of my mind? You know how illness upsets him."

Venetia's face became even more expressionless. "All dreams have a rational basis in past experience," she said. "What you need to do, obviously, is try to remember. . . ."

"Remember when I fell off a cliff on to someone's nasty face? You'd think I ought to be able to remember a thing like that without the help of a psychiatrist."

"No, but wait. You did have a cliff accident—don't you remember? When you were about five? When Fizz ran off—when you were with her at Penleggan."

"Penleggan? Where's that?"

"In Cornwall."

"Cornwall?" I stared at her blankly. "I'm sure I've never been to Cornwall."

"Oh, yes, I know you were there. I was in the Middle East then, running a refugee camp—it was before I took the Beirut job; I remember Fizz writing and saying you'd hurt yourself in a fall."

"Father would remember, maybe?"

"She might not have told him. It was probably in the middle of the divorce, remember; they wouldn't have been in touch. And he was ill. . . ."

"But if I had a fall, why don't I remember anything about it. Are there cliffs at this Penleggan place?"

"I've never been there. I might have a post card though . . . hold on."

An amiable, unexpected weakness in Venetia is her collection of post card albums. Within half a minute, she was back with a pile of bulky brown volumes.

" 'Fifty-five, 'fifty-four. Here we are."

I stared at my dead mother's faraway, long-ago handwriting, gay with spidery flourishes.

Darling Ven. Unbelievably happy if it weren't for poor Meggie. She is better but still a bit concussed. R. sends love.

"R.? Oh, Ralph, I suppose."

"He was in a West End musical about that time and used to fly down and visit her every weekend. The divorce came through in the autumn and they got married and took you off to Hollywood."

I turned the card over and stared at the picture. Beetling, faded brown, sepia cliffs sheered down to a huddle of white cottages.

"There certainly are cliffs. If I fell down there,

it's no wonder I got concussed. But what about the face?"

"Probably the oldest inhabitant picked you up, and because you were suffering from shock, his face upset you. Something simple like that."

"It sways to and fro," I said with difficulty. Even thinking myself into the atmosphere of the dream made me feel sick. "It sways to and fro for a long time, and then I see it again, *in another place,* and it's at that moment I know something perfectly dreadful is going to happen."

"All right, honey—take it easy now." Venetia patted my shoulder, and I realized that I was gripping the arm of my chair. "I'll tell you what: why don't you go down there, to Penleggan, and reenact the crime, or whatever they call it?"

"Chuck myself over the cliff?"

"No, but wander around and look at the place. Seeing it again—together with some peace and quiet and sea air—might undo whatever knot has got knotted up inside you."

"Oh no. No, I couldn't." Quickly I tucked the post card back into its slot. The very sight of those cuttle-fish-brown cliffs gave me goose flesh. "No, I'll be all right now, I expect. Just getting it off my chest to you has done me a lot of good. Probably by next month I'll wonder what I was fussing about. Don't they say there's no ill that matrimony can't cure?"

The evening wasn't a success. George was a bit preoccupied because of awful doings on the stock market during the afternoon. Polly arrived late, which didn't help, and I had the beginnings of a headache. Sitting through a variety show was the last thing I felt inclined for, but I could see that George was having feelings about the ruby ring, and if I seemed to criticize his choice of entertainment, that would just about put the lid on matters. Though what I did in the end was of course much, much worse: having sat doggedly through magicians, and comedians, and pop artists, when it came to the turn of a man who played three instruments while swinging on the end of a rope, I suddenly keeled over and found myself with my face on the collar of the man in the row ahead (he was very nice about it) and my feet all tangled under Polly.

George got me out and into the Citroën with the maximum efficiency while Polly patted and consoled me. However, driving home he was noticeably silent; I knew he was cross. At last, he said:

"If you were feeling ill, why come out?"

"I didn't know I was feeling ill. I thought it was just tiredness."

"I've told you you're overdoing the painting idiotically. You'll have to cut it down."

"Yes, George," I said meekly.

"I know exactly what we'll do," he said. "Tomorrow I can't, I've a meeting with the Royal Sunshine, important meeting that I can't possibly cut, but on Thursday I'll run you down to stay with Mutlets."

George's parents had retired from Rhodesia two years before and settled in Bournemouth to breed corgis. I didn't like his mother very much and found her self-chosen nickname regrettable, but it was none of my affair.

"Oh, thank you, George," I said, "but I'm sure your mother's too busy to have me. Besides, Hodge wouldn't get on with the dogs."

"Hodge can go to a boarding kennel; have to fix one up for him before we get married anyway."

"How do you mean?"

"Well, we can hardly take him on our honeymoon, can we?" George said reasonably. "So that's fixed. Pack your stuff tomorrow, I'll call for you on Thursday at half-past eight. Here we are—shall we come in?"

"No, don't, thanks," I said hastily. George's hatred of illness was making me feel guilty. Anyway, solitude was what I longed for, like a drink of cold water.

They got back into the car shouting good nights, and Polly called, "See you tomorrow." I went in.

I'd forgotten that I'd planned to stay the night with Venetia, but I was very glad I'd come home because Hodge was so pleased to see me. He stood on his hind legs and rubbed his whiskers against my hip.

I felt rather queer—not exactly weak, but as if my legs didn't belong to my head. Pottering about, doing my nails, having a bath, rolling Hodge's ping pong ball for him, I suddenly realized that I was trying to postpone bed as long as possible, and then the reason for this and for my general feeling of uneasiness came over me.

I was going to have the dream again. Two nights running. The whole atmosphere of my room suggested it—like a stage set before the actors come on. And the prospect was intolerable.

"Be blowed to this," I said aloud, and then wondered if talking to myself was the first step toward insanity. I picked up the telephone with the intention of ringing Venetia and telling her I'd be 'round shortly—it was still quite early, after all.

But in the space of time that it took to pick up the receiver—so quickly are decisions made, or rather made known, when our subconsciouses have been quietly working on them all the time—I discovered that I wasn't going to ring Venetia at all. With a sort of detached interest, I found myself asking for Information. There had been an address at the top of Mother's post card;

with a most unusual minimum of fuss my obliging sub-conscious produced it.

"Hullo, is that Information? Can you please give me the number of the Trevelyan Arms Hotel, Penleggan, Cornwall? Thank you very much."

Of course, the hotel won't have a room, I thought, while I was getting through to Penleggan with the same unnatural, movielike speed. Or else they closed down years ago.

But they hadn't closed, and they had a room. At first they said, doubtfully, that they didn't reckon to put people up much nowadays, but I was so persuasive that they finally agreed to have me.

"By the way, will you object if I bring my cat?"

"Cat, miss?" The pleasant, West Country voice sounded slightly startled.

"He's an Abyssinian. He's just like a dog, really."

"Fancy that, now! A cat like a dog!" There was a muttered colloquy in the background—evidently cats were something the Trevelyan Arms didn't regularly cater to—but in the end, the voice came back to say that would be quite all right. "We'll expect you tomorrow afternoon, then, miss. Good night."

"Good night," I said, jammed the receiver back on, and began hurling sweaters, and slacks, and sketch-books into a bag. Hodge watched me skeptically.

"It's all right," I told him. "You're coming, too."

Feeling rather like burglars we left the house and I got out the Mini I bought with the proceeds from my last four portraits—a pop group called the Buck House Boys.

So that is how it came about that Hodge and I were bowling, with a fine feeling of liberation and illicit adventure, down the Great West Road at about half-past one in the morning.

The road was beautifully empty. I was in no hurry, now I'd made my decision; I took it very comfortably, never over fifty.

At nine—we were in Devon by now—I stopped to buy buns for breakfast in a village called Little Hoe. I also sent two telegrams from its tiny post office, one to Venetia: "Following your advice re Penleggan," and one to George, "Taking short break in Cornwall. Will be in touch." I didn't give him the address because I didn't want a lot of fuss. Let him pry it out of Venetia if he must (and could).

After breakfast, I suddenly found that I was marvelously, blissfully sleepy. I turned aside down a rutted lane, turned again through a gate into a stubbled hay field. There was a haystack and also a big pile of straw from threshing. I pulled a rug and a cushion out of the car and curled up against the straw heap. Hodge curled up against me. In two minutes flat, I was fathoms deep in dreamless sleep.

When I woke, drowsy and relaxed, and looked at my watch, I could hardly believe my eyes. I had been asleep for over six hours; it was now after four.

I drove on faster now, gradually exchanging the rolling Devon hillsides for sharper, gnarled, treeless Cornish ups-and-downs. The whole countryside had a forlorn, windswept, ramshackle air. It was hard to imagine my gay, pleasure-loving, company-loving mother voluntarily coming to spend a holiday in this bleak part. But she was out to avoid publicity, Venetia had said.

However, Penleggan itself proved to be down in a deep cleft on the coast, and as I gradually descended the long valley road that led to it, I was relieved to find vegetation beginning again in the comparative shelter: first gorse, then thornbushes, then, as the road dipped deeper still, the real trees started, twisted and bent to be sure, with the fierce winds that blew off the Atlantic, but still dressed in their autumn gold; that queer, dead gold produced by the salt in the air.

I passed a couple of whitewashed cottages, both empty, a bungalow or two, and a few larger houses; then, the hill became much steeper and took a sharp hairpin twist to the right, another to the left, and I found myself in the middle of Penleggan. What there was of it. Half a dozen cottages lined a stone quay and the inn perched above them; a long building—warehouse or lifeboat station—stood at the back of a short pier. Beetling cliffsides enclosed the pint-sized harbor; I recognized the view in Mother's post card. In no other way was the village at all familiar; in fact, I felt a sort of resistance against it; I'd have been ready to swear that I never saw it before in my whole life.

Not a soul was about; the place seemed utterly deserted. The tide was half out and a stream of clear water trickled through a culvert under the road and briskly down between rocks into the harbor. I noticed that three or four of the houses on the quayside were standing empty and derelict, with broken, staring windows; a sunken boat lay disregarded, submerged to its gunwales in the green harbor water; Penleggan was a dead place.

But at least I knew that the Trevelyan Arms

had a landlord who answered the telephone; shivering slightly, and all at once aware of extreme hunger, I reversed the car, turned carefully, and worked my cautious way up the steep slope that led to the inn.

AN HOUR LATER, I WAS FEELING MUCH BETTER. I HAD had a massive high tea with eggs, and bacon, and cream, and jam while Hodge had been regaled on tinned sardines (no one seemed to have heard of fresh fish in this land of the pilchard).

I asked Mr. Vosper, the proprietor, if he had been here in 1954 when my mother stayed at the inn. No, he said, his dad had had the pub then; he had only left the Regular Army in '57, and sorry he was he ever came back to this dead-alive hole. He looked it: he was a thin, dark, scooped-out man with sad, opaque eyes. But if I liked, he added, he would fetch out the old visitors' book; I might find my mother's name in it. I did like, and he produced a fat blue book and then excused himself; someone had actually come into the bar.

I turned back through the stiff, scrawled pages until I reached the summer of 1954 and began looking for Frazers. It didn't strike me until I found myself staring at the name Smith in Mother's unmistakable, spidery flourish that she had been staying here incognito, keeping out of the way of the press and the Queen's Proctor, because though Father divorced her, Ralph was divorcing his wife. It had been a needlessly confused and messy business, Venetia had commented distastefully. Anyway, Mrs. Smith, London, was indubitably in Mother's handwriting. For further proof, under her name was printed a large and staggering MEG.

I stared at the page in baffled fascination, feeling

that it ought immediately to open a whole vista of memories. But nothing of the kind happened; my mind remained totally blank.

"Find what you wanted?" Mr. Vosper inquired kindly, coming back with a tray.

"Yes, thanks. I stayed here in September 1954."

"September '54?" he said, checking. "Why, that was when——"

"Walter!" his wife called from the kitchen. "Hurry up with the tray, dear."

"Coming, coming." He hurried away.

I decided to go out for a last look round before it became too dark. The sun had gone by now, but there was a pale, glowing light over the village that made it resemble a theatrical backdrop, neatly framed between the pincerlike cliffs. Hodge was asleep on my bed after his huge meal, so I left him there.

"Is there a road up the cliff on that side?" I asked an ancient, bearded man who was slowly stumping toward the pub.

He looked at me in silent surprise for a while; evidently a stranger was a rarity in Penleggan; then he said, "Oh, ay; but 'tis only a track, like, that leads up past Mr. Trevelyan's house." He pointed up and I saw that what I had taken to be a rock outcrop at the top of the cliff, outlined in black against the green sunset sky, was in fact a big house. As I looked at it, a window lighted up and shone yellow like a cat's eye.

"It's not a private road?"

"Oh, no, midear; that goo upalong towards Padstow, over the cliffs, past the Devil's Eggcup. But 'tis only a track, like."

"Can I take the car up it?" I asked, thinking there ought to be a fine view from up there. What was the Devil's Eggcup? I wondered.

"Oh, ay," he said after another period of reflection, "but that'll be praper devilish on tires, past Mr. Trevelyan's; you'm asking for a puncture, m'dear."

So I walked up.

The track was tarred and well enough kept as far as the big gates of the house on the cliff; after that, it deteriorated. I stopped at that point to take breath—the climb had been pretty steep—and to have a look at the house. A headland ran out here; there was a tree-lined dip on its southern face, and the house lay in this as snugly as a cat on a cushion. From below, I had thought it a new house; now, against the sky, I saw the unmistakable outline of sixteenth-century chimneys, slab-built and buttressed. The manor house, perhaps; if Trevelyans had always lived in it, that accounted for the name of the pub. The track skirted its grounds and then ran out towards the point; I followed it, though resolving to turn back in no more than ten minutes. I didn't want to find myself lost on strange cliffs in the dark. Particularly *these* cliffs. But it would be nice to get a glimpse of the sea, which I could already hear, and smell, and taste in the air. Up here on top, the land was still lit by a silvery sunset glow, reflected from sky and sea.

My path led on, the sound of waves grew louder, and presently, I began to see white things floating in the air. Gulls? Balls of thistledown? Wrong season for snow, too small for gulls, I thought; then, I saw that they were pieces of foam, about the size of my two fists together, apparently being blown up from the foot of the cliff. The grass and furze were covered with them, like strange, glimmering, weightless mushrooms. I caught one and felt it vanish in my hand, leaving nothing but a little sandy grit.

Conscious that my ten minutes must be almost up, I walked on fast. Then the path dipped down, protected on the seaward side by a low wall, and, looking over this, I had my first sight of the Devil's Eggcup.

At some time, there must have been a tremendous subsidence, not on the face of the cliff, but a little way inland. Probably, the sea had chewed out a cave down below, and then the roof of the cave had collapsed, leaving a sort of gigantic well in the headland. Leaning on the parapet, looking down into the darkness of the huge hole, I could hear, but not see, the water tossing about in the bottom. There must be an entrance for the sea down there; I could hear the crump and boom of waves hitting rock, and it was from here that the clots of foam continually blew up. What a place! The seaward rim of the well was just a narrow rock saddle at the cliff edge, covered in turf. Diametrically across from me were what looked like terraces and cultivated beds—the gardens of Trevelyan House, no doubt.

I was thankful I had not brought Hodge; since a kitten, he had been recklessly venturesome but tended to panic in high places, go rigid with terror, and stay there yelling piteously until someone (usually me) climbed up and rescued him. I didn't much care for the Devil's Eggcup myself so I went quickly on another twenty yards until I got a glimpse of the open sea, snoring and boring at the foot of the next headland beyond a little bay. Then, honor satisfied, I turned back, passed the wall encircling the Eggcup with eyes directed inland, and hurried down toward Penleggan.

The village, lit by four watery street lamps, was no livelier than it had been by daylight, but the lights gave it a sort of melancholy, picturesque charm; I strolled past the pub and along the quay, planning a series of sketches for tomorrow. A frail and dwindled ash tree grew in front of one of the two empty cottages and threw changing shadows over the pockmarked white walls.

Something about the shadows, the aspect, goodness knows what, gave me a queer turn; my memory did a sudden somersault and, with horror, I thought: I've seen that house before, I've been through that door, I've looked out through those windows.

I felt a mixture of familiarity and dread stirring in me; cowardice urged me to hurry back to the inn, have a hot drink, and bury my head in a book; but curiosity—and pride perhaps—countered this impulse. After all, I had come down here to try and dig out memory—like a buried splinter; what was the use of turning tail at the first prick of the needle?

I might have hesitated longer, but I felt a sudden soft and violent thump against my leg; it was Hodge, woken from his nap and come out to meet me, rubbing his muscular sides against me with enthusiastic affection. Absurdly, his company strengthened my courage; I walked up to the empty cottage.

Neat, little, three-sided bay windows stared eyelessly, their panes all smashed. At a closer view, I could see the whitewash was mildewed and peeling. The door, a stable-type in two halves, was broken; the upper half was in place, the lower dangled sideways.

With a feeling of now or never, I ducked through the gap left by the lower door and stepped into darkness. Hodge brushed past me and ran ahead.

Once inside, I had to stand still for a moment or two while my eyes grew accustomed to the dark. I could feel that the room I stood in was a small one; moving a few cautious steps, I stretched out my hand and touched the rear wall which seemed to be covered with a framework of little compartmented shelves such as those found in old village shops. How long had it been empty? Quite a while, to judge by the damp smell.

Groping on, I nearly fell out of my skin with terror when something hard shot away from my hand, then, as I instinctively let go, came back and struck me on the elbow; five heartbeats later, I realized that I had knocked against the back of a rocking chair. Cursing my jellylike nerves, I moved back toward the windows, now palely outlined; each had a window seat, probably inches deep in dust, but who cared? My knees felt weak with reaction, and I sat down.

And instantly, memory rushed back.

I could just see the shape of the little room now (Hodge was questing and pattering in the dark, on the scent of some prey), and the outline of the rocking chair showed dimly against the patch of lamplight. It was still in motion.

Superimposed on this was the image of fourteen years ago. *A place all shut in and dark, except for one little light.* There should be an oil lamp on a shelf, one feeble orange flame. And somebody in the rocking chair.

That was why the face swayed to and fro. . . .

. . . I was in pain, my head bleeding, something broken in my leg (the leg that gave me twinges sometimes in wet weather; I had occasionally wondered why); Mother had gone for help. I had had a fall—a bad fall. This was the nearest house, and somehow, she had carried me here, left me, and run on to telephone.

Why didn't the person in the rocking chair go for help?

I knew the answer to that almost before I had formed the question: it contained one of the main ingredients of the whole situation's horror: the person in the rocking chair was *unable to move.* I lay helpless on my seat; he sat helpless in his chair; and now something terrible was going to happen. . . .

Suddenly, I couldn't bear the place a moment longer. By now, I was so tense that when a small creature darted across the floor with Hodge in hot pursuit, I almost fainted. These old quayside cottages were probably alive with rats. I jumped up, calling Hodge to come, and blundered toward the doorway. My foot crunched through a rotten board and I stumbled; recovering, I ducked under the door and ran along the quay. Hodge came bounding after with erect tail, in the highest spirits.

The Trevelyan Arms, with its bright windows and sound of voices, seemed like a haven of security and welcome. While Hodge made off up the street, looking for more excitement, I put my head through the saloon bar door to ask Mr. Vosper if he could make me a hot milk with rum in it.

Only then did it strike me that I might look a bit odd: white and startled, probably with dust and cobwebs in my hair.

Mr. Vosper evidently thought so. He eyed me solicitously and said, "Are you all right, miss? Pardon me for saying it, but you look as if you had had a fright."

"No, I'm fine, thanks. Well, if I did have a fright, it was my own fault. I looked into one of those old empty cottages and some creature—I think it was a rat—almost ran over my foot. I can't stand rats, they always put me in a panic."

Not absolutely true, but it made a good enough excuse.

"Arr," said one of the three customers in the bar, a little white-haired gnome of a man, "Penleggan du be main full of rats."

"Ought to get in a rodent operative," another man—thickset, dark, with a shiny, expressionless face—put in gloomily.

Mr. Vosper gave a short, sardonic laugh. "In *this* neck of the woods? Don't make me laugh. Unless

55

you can get your gaffer to lay it on with one of his friends in the Council."

The dark man smiled thinly at this, which was evidently intended as a joke, then swallowed the rest of his drink and went out. The little white-haired man glanced at the clock on the mantelpiece and, remarking, "Well, well, bedtime I reckon, or you'll be lacking your letters tomorrow, my handsomes. . . ." a statement which left me completely baffled—also hobbled out.

There was now only one person left in the room. Warming my hands at the cheerful fire, I studied him covertly while Mrs. Vosper heated my milk. A young man, a bit older than me but not much over twenty-five, with odd, light eyes and a shock of brown hair. He looked faintly familiar; I wondered if I had seen his picture in some newspaper. He didn't look like an inhabitant of Penleggan, and yet, when I came in, he'd been talking to the other men with the ease of old acquaintance, and when Mr. Vosper brought me my posset to the fireside, they went on in low voices, apparently with something they had been talking about earlier.

"He'll never give way," Mr. Vosper said glumly. "I'm staying on here till the lease runs out because I can't find a soul to take it over, but when that day comes, in three years' time, you won't see me for dust. There's hardly a person under fifty in the whole village; how could there be? What could they do?"

"It's a damn shame!" The young man's voice shook, apparently with anger. "What right has he to kill the place stone dead like this? Every time I come back, it's worse; someone else has moved away. I suppose you've had plenty of tries at talking him 'round?"

"Dear, yes. So've the Trevannions. So've the Jagoes. So've the Hoskinses. Everybody has. If *you* can't persuade him, Mr. Toby, that's his own kith and kin, son of his own brother, is it likely anyone else can?"

A door slammed, a customer, coming into the public bar, shouted, "Walt!" and Mr. Vosper went away to attend to him.

The young man seemed to recollect my presence. He strolled over on the pretext of poking the fire, and I was aware of his slightly puzzled scrutiny.

"You must be fond of a quiet holiday?" he observed.

"Yes—I suppose I am." As I said this, I had a sudden depressing vision of George's ideal holiday: big hotel, casino, water-skiing, dancing every night, half a dozen congenial couples always around.

"Well, you'll certainly find peace and quiet in Penleggan," the young man said moodily. "If ever a place was killed by slow strangulation, this is the one."

"Why? What's happening here?" I thought of the empty cottages, the deserted quay.

"It's the old boy who owns the whole place; he's my uncle, but don't let us think of him more kindly on that account. He despises modern ways, industry and tourism, and so forth; he has a stranglehold on Penleggan. He won't let anyone new come in to start a shop or sell so much as a picture post card or a chocolate ice. He wants to preserve the place as it was in the nineteenth century."

"Well, I suppose it does mean the village is kept very unspoiled," I said doubtfully. "If people can earn their living in other ways."

"Unfortunately, the only alternative is the ancestral practice of wrecking." Toby's voice was dry. "The fishing industry died when the railway came to Camelford because other ports are more economically placed for marketing. And Uncle Mark won't allow any kind of light industry; I've been trying for years to persuade him to agree to a canning factory up in the old slate quarries—there are masses of sprats here, they could process them for pet foods and fish paste—but he won't hear of such an idea. Says it would ruin the character of the neighborhood."

"What a shame," I said warmly. "No wonder there are so many empty houses. It gives the place a sort of haunted atmosphere, doesn't it? I went into one—the white house on the quay with the half doors—and I—well, as I said, I was glad to come out again."

Was it my imagination, or did he give me an odd look? Perhaps it was just the reflection of the flames in his queer, light eyes.

"Haven't I seen your picture somewhere?" he said abruptly.

"It's possible," I said with reluctance. "My name's Meg Frazer."

"The teen-age Hogarth of our day. Of course. Penleggan is honored. Are you down here sketching?"

"No, just resting. I stayed here once before, in September 1954, and I thought I'd like to come back and see if it was still the same."

"September '54?" Now his expression was *definitely* odd. I remembered Mr. Vosper's reaction to the same statement. "How very——" Whatever he had been going to say he seemed to think better of it and stopped. "Oh, well," he ended lightly, "I don't suppose you'll find it's changed much in fourteen years. You must have been pretty young then—you've probably changed a good deal more yourself. I must be off. Good night."

"Mr. Toby gone?" Mr. Vosper said unnecessarily, coming back to find me alone.

"Yes. He doesn't live here, does he?"

"No, he's an engineer, Mr. Toby is, over at Plymouth. He lived here as a boy. His uncle, Mr. Mark Trevelyan, has the big house up on the cliff."

"Oh, now I begin to understand," I said slowly.

"And Mr. Mark's the one who won't allow people to start shops or factories?"

"That's right. It makes Mr. Toby mad, because his own father—that was Mr. Mark's twin brother and half owned the place with him—he had it planned to start a fish cannery, and the plans all came to nothing. And nothing can't be done till Mr. Mark dies. He never married, so Mr. Toby inherits then."

"Is he an old man, Mr. Mark Trevelyan?"

"Not he. No more than in his fifties, good for another score."

"So it may come too late to save the place. . . . What a miserable situation. But what happened to the twin brother, Toby's father? Why didn't he carry out his plans?"

"He was murdered."

"*Murdered?*" I said, startled. "How?"

"It happened when I was overseas," Mr. Vosper said. "Mr. Gerald was living on his own—his wife had died and Toby was away at boarding school. When he got wed, he and his wife converted two of the cottages in the village and lived there. Then one evening, he was found dead, shot right through the heart. They never found who did it."

"Wh. . . ." I found my voice was a croak, cleared my throat, and started again. "Which house was he murdered in?"

"Why, that empty cottage on the quay. The white one. It stood vacant for years after that, then a Truro man tried to run it as a tobacconist's. Mr. Mark gave him leave, to stop the stories about the place. But he didn't stay long."

"Why? What were the stories?"

"Oh, terrible nonsense. The usual sort. Folk said Mr. Gerald's ghost could be seen of a nighttime, rocking back and forth in the chair where he was sitting when they found him. . . ."

"Excuse me," I said shakily. "I suddenly find I'm very tired. I—I think I'll be off to bed. Thanks very much for the hot milk. Good night. . . ."

I DIDN'T SLEEP AT ALL THAT NIGHT. ON ACCOUNT OF my long nap earlier in the day, probably. I wasn't sorry to stay awake, either, for if I so much as closed my eyes, the swaying face of my dream rose up out of the dark and hung before me with its promise of catastrophe.

I kept the light on and read. Hodge presently arrived through the window, via an outhouse roof, and snoozed on my bed. When at last daylight began to show, I hauled a chair to the window, wrapped myself in a quilt, and watched the tide go out and the gulls quarrel on the rocks.

From where I sat, I could see along the quay to the dejected ash tree and just a sliver of the little white house with the broken door. Every time I dragged my eyes away from it, I found them slipping back. Someone called Gerald Trevelyan had been murdered in there, shot through the heart as he sat in a rocking chair. How long ago had this happened? And what, I wondered, had Gerald Trevelyan looked like?

It was when this question came to me that I found myself suddenly impelled to do something I had never thought of trying before: I pulled out a sketchbook and made an attempt to draw the face of my dream. Heaven knows it had dangled before me often enough.

Even so, getting it on to paper wasn't easy; there seemed such a basic difference between my dream-image and my struggles at reproduction that it was as if not one but a whole series of dimensions were missing. I almost despaired at first, scrapped dozens of efforts, and felt very little satisfied with the final one. Details such as the color of hair and eyes completely eluded me, but I thought I'd managed to catch the shape, and structure, and the expression of the face itself. . . . Something wasn't quite right, though. What did it lack, I wondered, what feature had escaped me? One thing I had caught, or so (perhaps subjectively) it seemed to me: even in my crude version, something of terror lurked, something unchancy.

I hoped that this putting it down in visible form would prove a sort of exorcism. At any rate, it had made me tired. At last, just as the first cocks were beginning to crow, I tumbled into bed and sank into blessed oblivion.

THE VOSPERS LET ME HAVE MY SLEEP, AND IT WAS nearly eleven before I staggered drowsily downstairs to a breakfast of surprisingly good coffee and hot Cornish buns. After breakfast, I wandered out on to the quay. It was going to be another hot, still, September day. I sat on one of those granite mushrooms—bollards?—and began sketching the little row of houses while Hodge alternately sunned himself on a pile of rusty chain or prospected beyond the broken stable door.

A voice from behind made me jump.

"Morning, midear," it said cheerfully. "Would this be for you, now?"

I turned and saw a stocky little postman with snowy white hair and black twinkling eyes. I recognized him as the gnomelike man who had been in the bar the previous evening. He had a game leg and must have been far past the usual age for retirement, but presumably, they didn't worry about such things in Penleggan. He was holding out a post card addressed to Miss Meg Frazer, c/o the Trevelyan Arms.

"We don't get many foreigners in the village," he explained, "so I reckoned 'twas you as must be Miss Frazer."

"Why, thank you." The card was from Venetia. It said:

> Keeping G. at bay in case you don't want to be pursued. He is a bit cross, though; suggest you compress research into fairly short space of time or else get in touch. Take care. Love V.

That made me feel guilty because it was surprising how much I was enjoying the freedom of *not* being in touch with George. I resolved to write to him tomorrow or, anyway, the very next day.

I looked up to find that the postman had limped across the quay and taken up a comfortable position on the next bollard. After exclaiming in polite amazement over Hodge, whose like, he said, had never been seen in Penleggan before, he added innocently, "You'll be from London, maybe?" as if he hadn't read the postmark.

"That's right," I said.

"Would this be your first stay in Penleggan, now?"

Not quite, I said. I had stayed here once before in September 1954, and waited for his reaction. It came.

"Why," he said, "you wouldn't be the little maid that—but, no, *her* name was Smith."

This was getting interesting. I said, "My mother's name was Smith. Mine's Frazer."

"Well! Fancy that!" His eyes shone, round with amazement. Evidently this was a bigger piece of news than Penleggan had had for many a day. " 'Tis brave of you to come back, then. The place won't have very happy memories for you, I'm afeared."

I decided to plunge right overboard. It didn't seem as if I'd ever have a better opportunity than this.

"But that's just the trouble," I said. "I don't have *any* memories. My aunt told me I'd had a bad fall at Penleggan, but I can't even remember that—can't remember being here at all. And my mother, who brought me here, died ten years ago."

"Arr!" he said again in astonishment. "Is that the truth, then? Old Dr. Menhenitt he said as how he reckoned the memory 'ud come back one day, and us often used to wonder about it. And it never did! Well! Isn't that a terrible thing!"

"Why. . . ." I was rather breathless. "Does that mean that *you* know? Can you tell me what happened? Were you here then?"

"Oh, ay, I been here or hereabouts for the last seventy years. Everybody in Penleggan knows old Nab Santo." He chuckled. "Saving when I was in one o' they submarines and got this." He patted his lame leg. "Oh, ay, I was here when you had your turnup, m'dear. Fell off them rocks out by harbor mouth yonder, you did, and broke your poor liddle leg, and knocked yourself silly. Your mother didn't like for to leave you where you fell, tide was a-making, you see, so she fetched you back herself, all the way, poor woman, so far as Mr. Gerald's cottage, and there she left you while she went

63

on to hospital. Praper good little cottage hospital we had that time, still, afore 'twas closed down."

"Is Mr. Gerald's cottage that white one there with the broken door?"

"Ay. Mr. Gerald Trevelyan, twin brother to Mr. Mark, he lived there. 'Twas the year after he got paralyzed."

"Paralyzed?"

"He went sailing with his missus, year before, time he come home on leave. Engineering, out in Argentina, that was his job. His owd boat sank—not properly laid up while he was away, they reckoned—his poor young wife was drowned, and Mr. Gerald never walked another step."

"So my mother left me in Mr. Gerald's cottage," I said breathlessly. "What happened?"

" 'Twas evening then," he said slowly. "All of a glim, like. I was just peglegging upalong to the Arms, for a pint, when I heard a shot. That's funny, I thinks, and I goes down to quay. Couldn't see a soul, but the way was dark; they'd no street lamps, then. No electric, for that matter. I goes in, and there's Mr. Gerald, dead in's rocking chair, shot clean through the heart, but, will you believe it, still rocking! Neighbors come runnin', course, but 'twadn't for a considerable time that we see'd the little child, as must have been you, miss, stiff out and fainted in the windy seat. You was took up to hospital, but when you come 'round you said never a word. Dr. Menhenitt reckoned as how with the fall you'd had, and the concussion, you couldn't 'a knowed anything about Mr. Gerald's murder, likely never saw a thing. He'd hardly let the police bother you wi' questions. And when you got better your mother took you away, no address left, and nobody knowed where you'd gone. But some of us used to wonder, like, if you'd seen what had happened and it had left you dumbstruck."

"It was definitely murder, and not suicide?"

"They couldn't find the gun, m'dear. 'Twas a bullet from Mr. Gerald's owd German pistol he'd brought back from the war, but find that pistol they never did, not to this living day."

"And they never discovered who did it?"

"Never," he said solemnly. " 'Twas a black mystery. Who'd want to hurt poor Mr. Gerald that never harmed a soul and was everlasting helpful to every mortal soul in the village? If it had been his brother now. . . ."

"Where was his brother, then?" I asked inquisitively. "Was he here too?"

"Ay, he'd been here all's life long. He never served in the war like Mr. Gerald did, because of's dodgy heart. Time o' the murder he was up to hospital, visiting his aunt, old Lady Trevelyan, and a-reading to her of's poetry, like. Mr. Mark's a terrible one for poetry. Every evening he used to read to her, and the finish o' that was, she left him ninety hunnerd pound."

"So he couldn't have done the murder?"

"Mr. Mark? Eh, no, miss!" The postman was slightly shocked. "Love lost atwixt the brothers there wadn't, account they had differing notions about the village, but blood is thicker than brine, say what you like. Why, time Mr. Gerald was found shot, Matron found Mr. Mark up to hospital, in Lady Trevelyan's room, passed out wi' a mortal heart attack, and the old lady sleeping like a babby. Some said it was a kind of sympathy as struck him down at the same moment when's twin brother was killed. Ay, he was in hospital himself for weeks after, poor soul."

"Goodness," I said, "what a dreadful thing. Is anybody from the hospital staff still living here?"

"Owd matron, owd Miss Pentecost, she be here still, retired, living up yonder."

"What about the doctor—Dr. Menhenitt?"

"Dead this many a year, poor soul. And so's many another. Ay, whoever killed poor Mr. Gerald, 'tis possible enough he'm gone to's own rest by now, and we'll never know."

After another ten minutes of innocently purposeful chat, designed to find out every last thing about me, the postman limped off.

By now, it was so unseasonably blazing hot that I decided to swim. I learned from the Vospers that there was safe bathing in a cove south of the harbor point, and Mrs. Vosper made me some sandwiches. Collecting swimsuit and sketchbook, I set off that way with a hope, too, of identifying the place where I had fallen and broken my leg.

Hodge elected to stay behind at the pub. Sardines and a comfortable bed, he indicated, were vastly preferable to hot and thirsty clamberings over hard rocks. I was rather relieved, on account of his poor head for heights.

A narrow path led round the south side of the harbor, sometimes dipping just below the high-water mark. Today, it was dry and well above water. I wondered what sort of weather it had been when Mother carried me back, with my broken leg and my concussion. Tide was a-making, I remembered old Nab Santo had said.

Across the harbor, high up above rock, and turf, and gorse, the Trevelyan house slept in its fold of hillside. It was an impressive building now that I saw it in daylight: granite-built, half farm, half manor, with what looked like the remains of an old chapel. I couldn't see the Devil's Eggcup, which must be directly beyond it, on the north side of the point. A blink of light caught my eye as I studied the house: probably somebody opening a window. I walked on, following the path which turned away from the harbor mouth now and climbed steeply over a shoulder of cliff.

And here, standing on the summit, I had another of those queerly unnerving jolts of memory. No need to wonder if this was the place where I had fallen; I *knew*, because it was the exact replica of my dream—the steep slope below the path, covered in loose, slaty shale, ending in an overhang beneath which lay an unguessable drop, and then, jutting out, a ridge of seaweedy rock.

I salute you, Mother. Father washed his hands of you, Venetia loved you but thought you a flibberty-gibbet; you were birdbrained, beautiful, maybe fonder of parties and acting than bringing up a daughter or being a devoted wife to a sick husband, but just the same, it took plenty of guts to get a hurt child up that cliff and along the harbor path to Penleggan.

We must have been coming back from the cove —which lay ahead, its sand a white and inviting curve, bare as a scimitar.

And then—the scream, the rattle of sliding stones, the moments of helpless horror, the crash. . . .

I found I was clenching my hands on the strap of my paint kit.

But I don't really mind heights—not actual heights in daylight—and soon I went on, confidently enough, past the patch of scree and down to the cove.

The sand was heavenly and hot; I bathed and basked, slept and ate, sketched a little, and bathed again. Time drifted past in an easy, meaningless way. I dressed, at last, but lingered, reluctant to leave.

Pulling out my sketch of the dream-face, I studied it curiously. Here, in the hot sun and the sound of the waves, it had lost its uncanny terror. It was just a face, any face.

I wondered if anybody in the village would be able to identify it.

What a curious, dreadful story that had been about the death of poor Gerald Trevelyan. And what a judgment on Mother. Poor Fizz, carefully choosing the smallest, remotest place she could find for her stolen meetings with Ralph, only to be plunged into the middle of an unsolved murder. It was lucky *she* hadn't been present at the crucial moment, or she'd have been landed with giving evidence. How glad she must have been, too, that she'd registered as Mrs. Smith. And that the defunct Dr. Menhenitt had proved such a redoubtable ally in preventing the police from badgering me. After all, what information could police hope to get from a concussed five-year-old child?

What indeed—except the image of a dream-face?

Absorbed in these thoughts, I had not heard the footsteps coming down the cliff path until they crunched over the shingle nearby.

I turned then and saw the young man, Toby Trevelyan, coming towards me. From my sitting position, he looked taller than I remembered. The expression on his face was strained and rigid; he was looking fixedly at my sketch of the dream-face which still lay on the sand beside me.

"Who did that?" he asked curtly as he came up.

I raised my brows to indicate that I found his behavior intrusive and unmannerly.

"I did, of course."

"Where? When did you do it?"

"Last night. I couldn't sleep, so I passed the time by drawing it."

"But I don't understand," he said. "Why? Why should you do such a thing?"

"*I* don't understand, either, I'm afraid. Why the inquisition? Can't I draw faces if I choose?"

"Why? *Why?* Because—that sketch you say you

did last night is a portrait of—of my father, who died fourteen years ago."

"Oh," I said limply. "Oh, I see. I'm sorry. How —how extraordinary."

But now that I looked at it, there was a sort of likeness between Toby's face and the one in my picture. No wonder he had given me that queerly familiar impression the night before. The similarity was not strong, but it was there—the same structure of cheek and jaw, temple, and the placing of the ear.

"Had you seen a picture of him somewhere— in a newspaper or something?"

"No, never, that I know of."

"Then——?"

"It's an awfully long story," I said. "Hadn't you better sit down?"

He dropped down beside me, leaning against a rock. His face was still taut, with puzzlement rather than hostility. "This has rather knocked me," he said. "It was such a shock—so unexpected. I was sent to ask you to dinner."

"Dinner?" I said stupidly.

"Properly chaperoned, of course." He gave a reluctant grin. "By now, thanks to the postman, it's all over the village what a notable young painter is regaling us with her presence, and my uncle commissioned me to come down and ask if you'd care to make a fourth tomorrow at his bachelor establishment with me and old Miss Pentecost."

"Miss Pentecost? The one who was matron of the hospital?"

He looked surprised, but nodded, and went on, "Uncle Mark gets catastrophically bored, you see; he can't lead an active life because he has a heart condition. He used to be a bit of a celebrity himself long ago."

"Oh yes?"

"Don't try to pretend you've heard of him because I'm sure you haven't." Toby shot me a satirical glance; he seemed to be recovering his poise. "Twenty years back or so Uncle Mark had quite a name for writing strictly British verses about strictly British things like scarlet pimpernels, and song thrushes, and thatched cottages, and chaps climbing Everest; he used to broadcast a lot, and have bits in daily papers (not weeklies, they were a bit above him), and publish endless, slim volumes that sold awfully well in our overseas colonies. But tastes changed, and Uncle Mark was left high and dry. . . . That was his first and last claim to fame, apart from keeping Penleggan as a sort of feudal hangover."

"I see. He sounds quite a character. Well, thanks very much, I'd love to come to dinner."

He gave me another satirical loog, and I added truthfully, "His house is beautiful; I'd love a chance to see inside it."

"Now," he said, "what about your story?"

"My story," I said slowly. "Yes, I suppose I owe you that. If you haven't already heard it from the postman."

"Only that you're the girl who started painting crowned heads at eigheen."

So I told Toby Trevelyan my story.

No audience could have been more flattering. He sat totally still, totally attentive, a disregarded cigarette slowly turning to a long column of ash between his fingers. When it burned him, he absently stubbed it out in the sand. His eyes never left my face.

"So you see," I ended, "it was like a locked cupboard—high up, out of reach in my mind—which needed opening and tidying before I got married."

"Yes, I see. . . . It didn't occur to you—no, how

could it, not knowing the story of the murder—that there's a sinister corollary to your locked cupboard simile?"

"How do you mean?" I asked cautiously.

"Why, that locked cupboards sometimes have skeletons in them. That there may be someone in Penleggan who isn't keen on your coming back here and trying to remember what you saw fourteen years ago? In fact, it's a lucky thing for you that the face which haunts you happens to be that of poor Father—who wouldn't have hurt a fly, incidentally."

"What are you getting at?"

I was grappling with a curious sense of panic. It should have relieved me to learn that my dream-face was that of the murdered man—the man in the rocking chair, swaying to and fro. It should have relieved me, but it did not. Why?

"What am I getting at?" said Toby. "Why, that the face you saw and remembered might equally well have been that of the murderer."

"Oh," I said. "Oh, I see. Yes. I hadn't thought of that."

"Do you know," Toby said, "quite honestly, I shouldn't stay here if I were you."

"You really think—oh, but that's absurd. Fourteen years ago—the people here will all be different, surely?"

"Some may have died," Toby said, "and some have moved away. But nobody new comes to Penleggan any more. It's a dying place. Everybody who lives here *now* lived here *then*. So I really think that you might be well advised to pack and go back to London pretty soon. It *was* a murder, remember."

I said inquisitively, "Wouldn't you be glad if it could be solved?"

"No," he said slowly. "No, I don't know that I should. Let sleeping crimes lie. It wouldn't bring poor Father back, would it?"

I sighed. "No, I see. Oh dear. I don't a bit want to go. It's so beautiful here."

"Isn't it? Have you seen the view from above the Devil's Eggcup?"

"Not properly in daylight. I went yesterday evening, but it was too dark to see much."

"I'll show you when you come up to dinner. There isn't a better sight in Cornwall. If only Penleggan could be brought back to life," he said passionately, "and the inhabitants given some means of turning an honest penny, it would be a perfect place. My God, what wouldn't I give to be able to do something. It makes me mad, absolutely mad, to see it rotting away. Heaven knows, I'm not crazy about 'Gifte Shoppes' and snack bars, but even they would be preferable to this slow decay."

"Mr. Vosper said you wanted to start a canning factory?"

"Yes I did, and it was quite feasible. I could have got the capital and the backing. I know several firms who'd be interested. And it would be the breath of life to a dozen families in the village—the whole area, if come to that. But I won't bore you with my hobbyhorse."

"No, but I'm interested. It's a good ambition—to bring a place back to life."

"It is, isn't it?" he said, his face lighting up at my enthusiasm. "With a bigger population, we could have a school again—nowadays, the children are taken off by bus twenty miles to Simonbridge, what children there are—clubs, evening classes, recreations—maybe a little theater, something that would draw summer visitors. Oh hell, though, what's the use of talking? Old Uncle Mark takes such care of himself, he's quite capable of living into his eighties. Not that one wants to hasten the old boy's end, but, my God, if it had been he and not my father who had been murdered, things would be very different here now."

"Tell me about your father's plans," I said, idly beginning to color in my sketch.

"D'you really want to hear?" Toby launched eagerly into a description of schemes for the improvement of Penleggan, schemes so sensible, moderate, and yet imaginative, that I was soon entering into his ideas and making suggestions of my own with as much wholehearted partisanship as he could have wished.

"Toby, it's wonderful! Let me know when you start, and I'll come and open an art school!"

"I'll keep you to that!" He grabbed my hands. "We'll knock Portmeirion for six—that is," he added, recollecting, "if we ever get the chance."

"And if George lets me," I said, with recollections of my own.

"George?"

"The man I'm going to marry."

"Oh," he said. "Oh, yes. . . . What does George do?"

So I told him about George and, one thing leading to another, about my father and Venetia, and my mother's story, and he told me how his uncle had brought him up after the death of his parents.

"Uncle Mark never married; I've an idea he secretly pined after my mother. I found a whole box full of photographs of her once in a drawer of his desk."

"I'm becoming more and more curious to meet your uncle."

A shade of reserve crossed Toby's face. He said,

"You'll dazzle him, I'm sure; all the old-world courtesy and charm will be turned on, ten kilowatt. Well, perhaps we should be hastening away to the mountain brow. At least I ought to. I've a date in St. Austell."

"Good heavens, I'd no idea it was so late. I'd intended to go and call on Miss Pentecost."

"I'll take you up and introduce you if you like," said Toby.

"But what about your date?"

"Only an old school pal; he won't worry if I'm fifteen minutes late. And it's on my way. I can go straight on."

With unceremonious friendliness, he pulled me to my feet. "Good lord, girl, you're as light as a feather. What do you live on—lettuce?"

TOBY'S BATTERED OLD TWO-SEATER STOOD BEHIND MY Mini outside the pub. Miss Pentecost, apparently, lived about a mile up the hill on the road out of Penleggan, so, as Toby was going on to St. Austell, I suggested we drive up separately. Toby led the way.

Hodge was asleep in the Mini. I used to leave the window open six inches when the car was in the garage at home, and then, if he couldn't find me, he'd get into it for company. He woke and greeted me affectionately.

In spite of its ancient appearance, Toby's car had powerful acceleration and shot up the steep hill like a bullet. I followed more cautiously in second, rounded a last hairpin curve, and found him parked on the right a bit farther up, outside a neat, green gate in a neat, green hedge. I had gone past before I could pull up, so

I went on, backed into a field entrance, and returned, parking my car below the two-seater, facing downhill. I left it in reverse for good measure; the slope was practically vertical.

Toby had already gone through the gate and was halfway up a long, grassy garden path, talking to a plump little woman with neat gray curls, and fending off the attentions of a frantically barking Pekingese. Hodge had nipped out of the Mini, intending to come with me, but when he saw the Peke, he retired into the hedge with a look of utter disapproval. He simply despised dogs.

Toby turned and waved to me. I walked up the path, and the little woman came forward with dignity.

Evidently Toby had already had time for a brief explanation. The ex-matron gave me a cheerful smile, studying me with shrewd blue eyes, and said:

"Well, now, you've grown since I saw you last, but I think, yes, I *think* I should have recognized you nonetheless. Same color hair and eyes. And I seldom forget a face."

"Good heavens!" I said. "But I was only five when you saw me last, Miss Pentecost!"

"Yes, my dear, but it was in somewhat striking circumstances, you must admit. I've often wondered how you got on afterward; after you left Penleggan, that is to say."

"Well," said Toby, glancing at his watch, "now I'd better be on my way or this chap who wants to sell me a dinghy will begin to think I've changed my mind. . . ."

Miss Pentecost was reproachful. "Over a year since you've been to see me, Toby, and then you only stop for two minutes! I'd hoped you'd come in and try my walnut-leaf wine."

"I daren't, Penny—I'd never get to St. Austell in one piece! I know your brews," Toby said laughing. "No, seriously, I must go, I'm late. Anyway I'll be seeing you both at Uncle Mark's tomorrow. Goodbye until then."

He held my hand for a moment, smiled at me, and then he was gone in a coughing roar from his old car.

"Well, now, this is nice," said Miss Pentecost. "An unexpected visitor in Penleggan is a real treat; we see so few."

"I gathered it's very quiet here nowadays." The Peke made running sallies at my ankles as I followed her along the grass path.

"Yes, yes. Toby, of course, would like to see tourism and industry brought here—*Ming*! behave yourself!—but, as I tell him, we must look at both sides of the question; unspoilt peace has its value, too. Now, this is my tiny house which Mr. Trevelyan kindly gave me permission to build when the hospital closed down and I retired; all this is his land, of course."

"Oh yes, of course." I guessed that, whatever her own opinions about Penleggan, it might be politic for Miss Pentecost, as a tenant of Uncle Mark's, to pay lip service to his views. "But I thought he wasn't keen on any new buildings going up?"

"No, he isn't, not at all," she agreed. "But as I had looked after his old aunt, Lady Trevelyan, for so many months—not to mention Mr. Trevelyan himself with his heart trouble—he very kindly made an exception in my case. I detest those damp old cottages."

Miss Pentecost was plainly devoted to her little house—a neat bungalow, white and slab-roofed, designed in keeping with the older houses below it. Both house and garden were exquisitely kept. I wondered who had done the pleasant watercolors on the walls. "It's *most* interesting that you've come back," she said, having put me firmly into a stout armchair. "With such associations it might have been the last place you'd want to revisit—but Toby tells me you still remember nothing of your previous experience here."

"No, not a thing. Isn't it queer?" I said, reflecting that Toby had told a lot in a short time.

"It isn't so very unusual," Miss Pentecost said tranquilly. "People's memories of childhood experiences are often very incomplete."

"Yes, but you'd think that such—such striking circumstances, as you called them, would leave some sort of trace."

"You really remember nothing? Not a thing?" She had been bustling around, getting out two tiny crystal glasses and a decanter polished to sparkling perfection; now she paused, decanter in hand, and eyed me sharply.

"Not a single thing. Apart from this dream I have of a face—which Toby tells me is his father's. Otherwise, I'd be prepared to swear I'd never set foot here before—if it weren't for the evidence of Mother's and my names in the hotel register. But since. . . ."

Since I've come back, memory has started to prick through, I was going on to say, but Miss Pentecost had spilt a drop of walnut wine on her shining tabletop and, scolding herself under her breath for her own clumsiness, bustled out to the kitchen for a cloth.

"That is very interesting," she said when she came back. Absently, she poured from the decanter; absently, she studied the little glass of greenish liquor, holding it up to the light. "Do you think it *really* wise," she went on, "to come down here now and stir up all these buried troubles?"

Her disconcertingly sharp eyes were fixed on me

intently; was she administering a warning as Toby had done?

Even if she was, I resolved to disregard the warning. I had come much too far, now, to draw back.

"Yes," I said firmly. "I'm sure I ought to do it. You see, I've been having these nightmares, worse and worse. . . . I feel it's like a scar that healed over too soon; the bullet's still in the wound."

The minute I had said this I thought how melodramatic it sounded; Miss Pentecost seemed quite startled and considered me in silence for another moment or two before she said at length, rather abruptly, "Yes. Yes, I suppose so."

"Won't you tell me what *you* remember about that business, Miss Pentecost?" I urged her.

She sighed. "Well, you seem a sensible enough girl. All right, my dear." She crossed the room and put the little liqueur glass down beside me. "Try this: walnut-leaf wine, my own make."

"It won't knock me under the table, will it?" I said laughing. "I've got to drive down Penleggan hill, remember."

"Oh no, my dear, that was just Toby's nonsense."

Nevertheless, I sipped cautiously, but the stuff tasted mild enough, bland with the faintest aromatic flavor. "Very good," I said politely.

"It is, isn't it? Oh dear, there are my groceries arriving. Excuse me just a moment. . . ." and she trotted out as a shadow passed the window and a knock fell on the door. She was some little time returning, and I had leisure to study the watercolors and a whole series of photographs, evidently the staff of the Cottage Hospital.

"And that's that," said Miss Pentecost, coming briskly in again. "Let me fill up your glass—oh, no, you *must*, it's such a tiny glass—and then I'll tell you what I can remember."

"It was in September 1954, wasn't it, that you and your mother came to stay? So pretty, she was. I often wondered if she was on the stage."

"Yes, she was," I said. "She went to Hollywood soon after. But she was killed in a car accident when I was nine."

"Ah, poor dear. That must have been a sad blow to you, child.

"You had been staying at the Arms for a week or two when one evening—I remember it was during visiting hours, the day staff were just going off duty— your mother staggered into the hospital in a state of collapse—in fact, she fainted on the office floor, and we had to bring her round. Then she told us you'd had a bad fall on the cliff at the harbor mouth, and she'd had to carry you all the way back to the quay; otherwise, the tide would have come in and covered the path before rescuers could get to you. She'd left you in one of the cottages."

"Wasn't there a phone anywhere?"

"She could have phoned from the inn but it was just as quick to come straight here. Of course, Mr. Gerald Trevelyan, whose house she left you in, couldn't walk."

"Where was the hospital?"

"Halfway down the hill. It's derelict now. Well, as soon as we heard what had happened, and where she'd left you, I started down toward the quay with a couple of nurses and a stretcher. We found about a dozen people in front of Mr. Gerald Trevelyan's cottage, and old Nab Santo in the doorway, trying to keep them out while he shouted for somebody to get the constable. We went in and found Mr. Gerald shot dead in his chair. But Dr. Menhenitt said, when he arrived, that it couldn't have happened more than ten minutes before. And then we found *you*, unconscious, with a bump on your head and a broken leg, on the window seat. You didn't come 'round for two days; quite worried about you we were, and then the doctor had you under sedation for several more, partly, I think, to protect you so that the police shouldn't start bothering you too soon."

"*Did* they question me?"

"An inspector came from St. Austell, but Dr. Menhenitt stayed with you all the time and so did your mother; and of course, they found that you couldn't remember anything at all, so that was the end of that. And there was no question of your giving evidence at the inquest. We had your mother in bed for several days, too, badly shocked, and not surprising; she'd carried you the better part of two miles and all the last part of the way, along the harbor path, halfway to her knees in water. It was a spring tide. Old John Vosper saw her, Walter's father that was; he was on the cliff, across the harbor, and hobbled along to help, but he was so old and rheumaticky that by the time he got down she'd vanished; she must have left you at the cottage already and gone on. He said it was a miracle she didn't slip and fall or get washed away. Then he heard a shot, and saw Nab waving from Mr. Trevelyan's door.

"Yes, that was an evening! We'd no sooner got you into bed than the police sent up to ask was Mr. Mark at the hospital, so I went along to his aunt's room, old Lady Trevelyan, and there she was, fast asleep, and Mr. Mark on the floor in a dead faint. Dr. Menhenitt was very interested; he said it must be a case of sympathy as they were twin brothers. He'd fainted at just about the same moment that Mr. Gerald was shot. So we had him as a patient too. . . . He was very sorry for you and your mother, used to send you grapes, and would have visited you, but Dr. Menhenitt thought the quieter you were kept, the better. I believe Mr. Mark wanted to get in touch with your mother after he was allowed out, but she'd taken you away by then and left no forwarding address.

"And that's really all I know, my dear!"

"It is mysterious, isn't it? I wonder who did do the murder and what happened to the gun."

"There was a verdict of murder by persons unknown," Miss Pentecost recalled. "For a time, Penleggan was quite a notorious spot; tourists used to come and stare, but when Mr. Mark was about again he soon put a stop to that."

"Well, thank you very much indeed," I said, rising to go.

The room lurched a little, and I realized with dismay that Miss Pentecost's walnut-leaf brew must have been far stronger than I thought; in fact, it must have had the kick of a mule for two tiny glasses to do this to me.

Perhaps fresh air would help.

I started cautiously down the grass path in the twilight, while the Peke let out a final salvo of barks.

"Do drop in again before you leave Penleggan," my hostess called cheerfully. "—Ming, be quiet!—We must have a chat about art. Someone said you painted; I'm by way of being quite a painter myself."

"Thanks, I'd love to. Anyway, I'll be seeing you tomorrow night at Mr. Trevelyan's, shan't I?"

"Oh yes, of course. That will be nice." Did she sound a little skeptical? She gave a last brisk wave, called Ming inside, and I heard the front door slam. Hodge stalked somewhat aloofly out of the hedge and whipped into the car as I opened the door.

Switching on the lights, I pulled the starter. The car gave a violent lurch; feeling a fool, I remembered that I'd left it in reverse. This checked my usual starting routine. I swung the gear shift back to neutral, shoved the window right down, and sat still a moment to try and shake off the effects of Miss Pentecost's knockout drink.

Then, feeling, I thought, reasonably clearheaded, I reached once more for the starter. As I did so, something large scrabbled over my foot. For an instant, I assumed it was Hodge—but he was in his usual place on the front passenger seat. I'd released the hand brake to start the car rolling—now I jerked it violently back again. The Mini swerved sideways and came to rest at an alarming angle across the road, front tires jammed against the curb. In the same moment, all hell broke loose inside, down on the car floor in the semidark. Hodge had hurled himself like a bomb on whatever was there; I could hear him growling fiercely, and a series of thuds as well as enraged squeals from something else, and a general scurry and turmoil.

I flung open my door and shot out, turning as I did so. The inside light came on as the door opened, and I saw a creature whip over the sill—something large and smooth. Hodge was after it like lightning, there was a final, fierce scuffle in the road, a final, piercing squeal, and then Hodge triumphantly shook whatever it was and threw it over his shoulder. It fell with a thud into the beam of the headlights; I stepped warily nearer and saw a huge gray rat, whose body alone must have been about eight inches long. Hodge growled at me as I approached it.

"All right, keep your fur on. I'm not going to confiscate your winnings," I said rather shakily, and got back into the car. Hodge gingerly inspected his prey again, gave it a final shake, decided he didn't want to eat it, and jumped back in beside me, shuddering his sandy coat all over as he does when thoroughly aroused.

I didn't start the car at once. I straightened it by the curb, checked carefully with the door open that nothing else was inside, and then sat back and took some deep breaths. It had been a *very* large rat. And how in heaven's name had it got into the car?

Could it have got in while the Mini was parked down on the quay? No, I thought, Hodge had been in the car then; that was out of the question.

Hodge growled again softly, licking a wound on his leg. "Are you all right, you old cuss?" I said, rubbing his head, resolving to swab him with disinfectant as soon as we got back to the pub. "I was lucky *you* were with me, anyway."

For the first time, then, it really struck me how lucky I was. Both for having Hodge with me and for having left the car in reverse. Without that, I'd probably have started straight into second gear on that steep slope, and been rolling briskly down the hill when the rat bumped me; there was a strong chance that I'd have swerved, and panicked, and run straight into a wall or over the outside of a hairpin curve, landing on somebody's roof down below. Specially with my reactions slowed and made muzzy by Miss Pentecost's walnut wine.

I hate rats.

No muzziness remained now. I was as sober as stocktaking day. I had made that remark recently. When, and in whose hearing?

It had been last night, I remember, in the bar, in front of three people—Nab, and Toby, and the unknown dark man. Was Mr. Vosper there, too? I tried to think. Was it possible that someone had deliberately put the rat into my car, either to frighten me away or to put a drastic stop to the chance of my asking awkward questions?

If so, then who?

I had been with Miss Pentecost about an hour; plenty of opportunity for anyone to nip up from the village while we were talking. Or, for Miss Pentecost herself to do it. I recalled she had left me alone for quite a long time while she was taking in her groceries. But why should she do such a thing? Where would she get a rat from? On the other hand, she didn't know that I happened to travel with a cat. Hodge had kept out of the way during my call. The dark man last night hadn't seen him, either. Nor—now I came to think of it—had Toby Trevelyan. But somehow, I found myself shying away from the notion that Toby might have left his two-seater farther up the hill and quietly sneaked back to put a rat in the Mini while I chatted with Miss Pentecost.

The thought of *anyone*'s having done it on purpose was unpleasant enough.

Presently, I started up once more and—once bitten, twice shy—crept down the steep hill in low gear with headlights blazing into Penleggan and parked outside the pub. Then I shut and locked the car.

Mrs. Vosper served me an excellent meal in the little parlor.

Afterward, I dripped antiseptic over Hodge's wounds, had a bath, and tumbled thankfully into bed.

For a moment, a face floated before my eyes— not my dream-face, but that of Toby Trevelyan, taut and strained as it had been when he first saw my sketch, with that odd look in his eyes. But if there was one person among those I had met in Penleggan who was incapable of having murdered Gerald Trevelyan, it was his own son, a boy of ten and away at boarding school when it happened.

Firmly, I put him out of my mind, drifted into sleep, and dreamed neither of cats, rats, cliffs, nor anybody's face at all.

NEXT DAY WAS GOLDEN FAIR, STILL WITH THAT INCREDI-
ble halcyon calm. I drank my coffee in the Vospers' little
slip of a garden, with its wizened, stunted apple trees,
overlooking the harbor. The tide was ebbing, nearly full
out, and the stream meandered down the rocks with a
gentle, trickling noise; reflections hung idle-still in the
emerald water across the harbor; even the gulls sat
motionless as a row of clay pigeons on the moss-grown
stone launching ramp.

I fetched a bowl of water and disinfectant and
bathed Hodge's wounds again. While I was thus at work,
Mr. Vosper strolled out. His gloomy face creased into
its difficult smile.

"Been in trouble?" He nodded at Hodge. "We
do have some tough old toms in these parts."

"This was no cat, it was a rat!" I said, and told
him about it.

Mr. Vosper was gratifyingly startled at my story,
and impressed with Hodge's prowess—though I suspect
he thought I was laying it on about the size of the rat.

There came a pause. Then, Mr. Vosper scraped
dolefully with his fingernail at a rust patch on the small
iron coffee table and whistled between his teeth. Looking rather embarrassed, he asked:

"Can you tell me how long—that is, when you'll
likely be leaving, Miss Frazer?"

I was rather taken aback. "Why, I'm not sure. I
hadn't thought about it, really. Is it—do you want my
room?"

This seemed most unlikely, since I had noticed three or four empty rooms besides mine, but Mr. Vosper said, "Yes, that's it," in a tone of relief, as if such a simple reason had not actually occurred to him.

"Oh dear, I see. Well, will it be all right if I stay until tomorrow?"

"Yes," he said doubtfully. "Yes, that will be quite all right. I'm very sorry, Miss Frazer, I don't want to seem unwelcoming or—or—hurry you off, but you know how it is, when it's a definite prior booking—we don't get so many of those. . . ." He was gabbling rather distractedly.

"Oh, no, I quite understand," I said. "Well—I'd better make the most of today, hadn't I? Anyway, this marvelous weather can't last forever."

I fetched my drawing things and sketched for an hour or so. I don't do much thinking, consciously, when I'm at work; my mind is a peaceful blank except for the messages that are being automatically transferred from eye to hand. I drew and drew, stopping only to sharpen sticks of charcoal, blow on fixative, or tear off a sheet of paper and start a new sketch. But presently, when I paused for a breather and to stretch my stiff fingers, the conversation with Mr. Vosper repeated itself in my brain like a tape recording that someone has been patiently waiting to play. Why was the landlord so uneasily anxious to get me out of my room? He had not seemed anxious until he heard the story of the rat, it occurred to me. . . .

Beneath its oasis calm, Penleggan was not a tranquil place. There were curious undercurrents, hidden tensions which I seemed to be stirring up; perhaps Mr. Vosper was right, and I would do better to leave. But, I thought suddenly, rebelliously, it was not in *my* interest to leave. If I was bad for the place, that wasn't my fault; it was good for me. I felt much calmer, more alert and relaxed than I had been for months. Venetia had been right in her view that a return to Penleggan would help me. Unless it was just being away from George. I realized that for two days I had hardly given him a thought.

Old Nab, the postman, came limping along the quay to say good morning.

"Handsome!" he exclaimed admiringly at my sketches of the forlorn little house. "Proper job! You'm fare to do some in color, m'dear, like they do have in the shops over to Padstow; sell like hot cakes they would, in liddle white-wood frames."

"I'm just doing this for fun," I said, laughing. "As a souvenir in case I forget the place again when I leave it, the way I did last time."

"Arr." He nodded approvingly. "Leaving tomorrow, ben't you?" Evidently, the news had already got 'round. " 'Tis only sense, too, weather changes powerful sudden this time o' year. And old Moggy there might get in more trouble——" He waved a hand toward Hodge, stretched in the sun, swatting floating thistledown with a lazy paw. "Been tanglin' wi' rats, I hear? There's plenty big brutes of rats in Penleggan—you'm wise to take him back where he'll be safe and sound."

Was this a warning? I gave him a sharp glance. But he was gazing vaguely out at the slice of sea visible through the harbor entrance, and he added, "Ay, 'tis faring up for a blow tonight, reckon; I mun slip round my lobster pots 'sarternoon, time Mr. Vosper'll be giving you a lobster to your tea."

I laughed. "Too bad—I'm having dinner up at the big house. Do you suppose Mr. Trevelyan will give me lobster?"

The news seemed to startle old Nab; his white gnome's eyebrows shot up into the fringe of hair on top. But he only said, "Well, now, fancy that, indeed," in a noncommittal tone, nodded as if his mind were suddenly on other matters, and stumped off along the quay.

I'm getting fanciful, I thought, gathering my sketches together, starting to imagine sinister overtones in every harmless conversation. Nab couldn't really have been shocked at my news. What could be peculiar or alarming about a dinner party with Mr. Mark Trevelyan at the big house, properly chaperoned by Miss Pentecost and nephew Toby? Probably, the old boy would be rather tedious; he might try to wheedle me into doing his portrait, but I was adept by now at dodging that; and I liked Miss Pentecost, and Toby—Toby was fun; it gave me a little warm feeling of pleasant anticipation to think that I would be seeing him again before I left.

I decided to try an interior sketch, and undid the laces of my portfolio to put away the completed drawings. Then I paused, puzzled and surprised.

I'm meticulous about the order of the sheets in my portfolio. And I was quite certain that I had left the colored portrait of the dream-face, Toby's father, at the very front, on top of an accumulated pile of other drawings. Now, it was not there. I hunted swiftly through the contents; then again, more carefully. But my search was fruitless. The portrait had gone. Could I have left it on the beach, in the car, in the parlor, upstairs in my bedroom? I thought back in detail over my movements yesterday and clearly remembered sliding the picture into the portfolio when I left the beach with Toby. He had carried it back for me. Then, before going up to Miss Pentecost's, I had slipped into the inn to tidy up and left the portfolio on the piano in the parlor. This morning it had been there, apparently undisturbed. But? Had somebody abstracted the portrait while I was at Miss Pentecost's? Or during the night? Why? It seemed a totally pointless thing to do, I thought, annoyed. Anyway, I could always draw the face again.

Still pondering over this enigma, I went into the little white house, ducking under the broken half door, without any of the feelings of superstitious apprehension that had shaken me the other night. Today, it was just a little house, damp, and in rather a bad state of disrepair. I wondered why it hadn't been kept up. Presumably, it belonged to Mark Trevelyan. Or Toby. Perhaps, they had feelings about it. Or perhaps, local workmen would not touch it.

In the cheerful morning light, it seemed harmless enough. A square of sunshine disclosed the crumbling worm-eaten state of the floor and dust motes dancing as I moved about. I could see my own tracks from two days earlier, the hole where I had put my foot through the floor, and the patch rubbed clear where I had sat on the window seat.

It seemed hard to believe that a murder had been done here—a human life snuffed out abruptly in this little room *in my own presence*.

Suddenly, I thought of Father, off in Liverpool, lecturing about bilharzia. How morbid he would find all this, how much he would disapprove of my coming back here to try and disentangle a blocked memory out of my childhood. I could imagine his skeptical expression, his chiding comment, "Really, Meg, isn't all this a bit melodramatic? How can you really imagine it will be any help, this sort of hysterical brooding over the past?"

I was glad that Father had been away when I decided to set off for Cornwall. And then it occurred to me to wonder whether—if Father had been more sympathetic when I was small, if he had ever talked freely to me, and encouraged me to talk to him, and tell him my troubles—these frightening memories would not have been driven underground, would not have returned in the form of dreams.

Not that there was much point in speculating

about it now. Father was Father, withdrawn and cautious, as life had made him. All I could do was promise myself that any children I had would be so encompassed with love and security that no nameless terrors would haunt their bedsides. I smiled a little, ironically, then, thinking that any children of George's would probably be cheerful, unimaginative young citizens, not at all subject to nameless terrors; I hardly needed to worry about them in advance. But this train of thought led to another, rather troubled, speculation: had my early engagement to George, that solid, dependable shoulder, that rock of security, been a further outcome of my unhappy, fear-ridden childhood? Obviously, it had, I thought uneasily; I had clutched him like the proverbial straw. Was this really fair to George? Was the vague build-up of resentment I now felt against him an expression of my subconscious knowledge that I had allowed us both to drift into a false situation?

Firmly dismissing these unprofitable thoughts, I set to work once more.

After I'd been drawing for about twenty minutes, the sun had moved and no longer shone through so that, in contrast with the cobbled quay outside, the small room seemed filled with dimness.

By accentuating the shading in my sketch, I produced the effect of evening, of dusk; a few extra scribbles hatched on the window seat suggested the huddled form of a child. . . . The sky must have been pale but clear outside, I thought; green and gold traces of sunset still lightening the western sky, a few stars beginning to prickle out overhead.

And then somebody had looked in through the window, blocking the opened lower half with his head and shoulders.

Had anybody told me that Gerald Trevelyan was

shot through the window? I couldn't remember. Whether they had or not, I knew that was how it must have been. It would be so easy to lean in over the small sill, to see the man in the rocking chair, illuminated from the side by the soft orange light of the oil lamp, a perfect target. The child on the seat under the window, motionless, huddled in shadow, would be easily overlooked.

My heart beginning to thump a little with excitement, I started lightly sketching in the shape of a man in the square of window: his hands, his forearms, elbows, shoulders, the outline of the face. . . .

"Hello!" said Toby, leaning in through the window. "So that's where you've got to! How are you today? I wondered if you'd like to come with me to one of our local beauty spots this afternoon—as I gather you're leaving tomorrow?"

I had started so violently when he first spoke that my hand jerked across the sketch pad and a jagged black line ended in a snap as the charcoal broke; I retrieved the broken bit and said composedly:

"Why, thank you, Mr. Trevelyan. I'd like that very much."

"Oh, do call me Toby," he said. "Mr. Trevelyan sounds like Uncle Mark."

"All right, Toby."

He swung himself under the half door, looked quickly round inside, and said with a shiver, "This place gives me the horrors. If it was mine, I'd pull it down. Why don't you come along out into the sun—if you've finished?"

"Oh yes, I've finished," I said. My drawing mood was broken. I followed him out.

"It belongs to your Uncle Mark, then?" I said as we walked away.

"Yes." There was a flat finality in Toby's voice,

discouraging further discussion. "How did you get on with Miss Pentecost?" he went on, in quite a different voice. "Isn't she an old duck? I ought to have warned you against her drink, though; sometimes it's about ninety percent proof. Were you all right?"

"Yes—thank you." I didn't feel inclined just now to tell him about the rat. "She was awfully nice. But she didn't really tell me much that I didn't know already. Where are we going?" I added, as he led me briskly along the quay.

"I want to show you this place called Merlin's Cave. My father used to take me there when I was small. It ought to be jam for a painter, you get the most amazing greens and blues, not to mention the colors of the rock."

"It sounds wonderful. Should I bring swimming things? And do we walk or go by car?"

"Neither. I'm borrowing Walt Vosper's motorboat. And, yes, bring swimming gear. There's a marvelous stretch of beach—untouched by human foot. I've asked Mrs. Vosper to put us up some lunch."

"You seem to have it all organized," I remarked coolly, but Toby only gave me a confiding grin and said, "Yes, haven't I? Special treat for your last afternoon. It really is a good place." He looked so ingenuous that I suppressed a half-formed notion of his having organized the excursion to keep me out of mischief.

"Walt says you travel with a tame cat," he went on. "Do you want to bring him?"

I definitely wasn't equal to the anxiety of taking Hodge in a boat—nor did I think he would enjoy it—so while I was collecting my swimsuit and towel, I shut him in my bedroom with a bowl of water and asked Mrs. Vosper if she would be so kind as to feed him, supposing we were not back by six.

"I'll take you out this evening," I promised him. "Settle down, now. You'd hate it, honestly," and he gave me a baleful look before starting to wash his undercarriage as an indication that he couldn't care less where I went or what I did.

Toby was stowing the picnic basket in a shabby red-and-white motor dinghy when I went out.

"It takes about an hour to get there," he said, looking at his watch. "High tide is at five so we'll have time to look at the cave and two or three hours on the beach before it gets covered."

He helped me in and slipped off the painter.

"Which way is this place?"

"Westward down the coast toward Newquay. You can't get there except by boat—that's why it's so good. It's too far to walk along the beach between tides. It isn't a cove—just a cave in the cliff face."

"There's no way down the cliff?" I asked as we chugged noisily out of the harbor against the first stir of the tide. Above us, to the right, Trevelyan House lay somnolent in its fringe of trees. To the left, as we rounded the point, I saw the slope of scree where I had fallen, the cove where I had paddled and played beside Mother . . . .

"Down the cliff?" said Toby, twirling the wheel. "Not a hope—unless you're a professional. It's too sheer all along this coast. No, boat's the thing. You get a nice view, too."

You did. Headland after headland rose, stark and impressive, stretching away to the west, the green of cultivated fields inland giving way to gold-brown bracken and gorse on the seaward slopes. And below the bracken, sheer, black rock ran down vertically to a thin, white line of sand.

"Not a crowded beach," I remarked.

"Nice, isn't it, to see sand without humans all over it."

"I'm surprised," I told him. "I should have thought you would yearn to install beach lifts down the cliffs, and paddling pools for toddlers—and deck chairs and a pier or two. . . ."

"Oh, come off it!" Toby grinned at me. "All I want is a decent living for people who happen to prefer to stay in the place where they were born. I'm not crusading for beach pavilions or bingo halls, as you know perfectly well. It would be rather fun to build a cliff railway, though, at that," he added reflectively. "Hydraulic—you fill a tank full of water at the top and down she goes; meanwhile, the other car comes up from the bottom. Like buckets in a well."

I asked him about his job, and he told me a bit, and then we got to swapping views on books we had read and films we had seen; the trip passed like lightning. In no time, I was helping haul the boat up onto a steeply shelving, narrow strip of white sand below the cliff. Then Toby showed me the cave.

Actually, I'm not crazy about caves, though I hadn't said so, as Toby seemed so keen to show me this one. There's something about cold, rocky, damp, shut-in places that comes altogether too close to my dream for comfort. So, although it was a fine specimen of a cave, with an arched roof like a gothic church and, as Toby had said, wonderful color effects of water and rock, I wasn't sorry to come out of its chill vaults into the hot sun again. We swam, then, and had a late lunch, and talked a lot more, and I reflected idly how queer it was to be on such easy terms with a person of whose very existence I hadn't been aware two days before. George would hardly approve, I thought.

Talking, and swimming, and dozing on the sand

was idyllic, but late September is not July, and the north coast of Cornwall is not the Riviera; presently, the cold shadow of the cliff crept down to our backs as the sun sank lower, and I said, "Toby, shouldn't we be thinking of going? The tide's nearly up to our boat, and it's getting a bit chilly."

"Yes, of course," he said quickly. "Sorry—are you cold? I'm always so happy when I come to this place that the time seems to float past—particularly today," he added with great simplicity.

"No, I'm not a bit cold. And I've had a marvelous time. But I was brought up inland—I get into an idiotic panic at the thought of being cut off by the tide." I glanced along the coast; already, in both directions, white frills of foam had begun to break at the cliff foot; only our little shelf of beach was left.

"Perfectly okay," Toby said reassuringly. "All we have to do is get in the boat and go. I'll just toss in the picnic things first then give you a hand."

We climbed in, barefoot and sandy, and turned for a last look at the beach. It was almost gone now; above it, deep in shadow, the cliff loomed black and formidable; the cave entrance looked no more than a fold in the rock.

"You must know this coast awfully well," I said. "I'd never be able to find that spot from the sea. It's a lovely place; thank you so much for bringing me. I've really—what's the matter?"

"I don't know," he said, frowning, pulling the engine cord. "It can't be anything much. Usually, Walt's boat starts like a bird." He tried again, once, twice, half a dozen times—then took off a hatch cover and began to tinker worriedly with the engine.

"Can I do anything?"

"Keep us fended off, could you?"

He passed me a boat hook. It was time. Waves had now rolled right over the beach and our insubstantial-looking craft was tossing nearer and nearer to the razor-ribbed rocks at the cliff foot. I hung over the side and fended with a will. Toby went on tinkering and muttering.

"*That* seems all right—and that; it's a decent little engine, nothing wrong there."

"Well," I said tentatively, thinking how George would have snubbed me, "could we have run out of gas?"

"Hardly. I filled her up before we started. I'll check the tank, though, just to make certain. Could you pass me that thing there? It's what Walt uses for a dipstick." I passed it. A moment later, Toby exclaimed, "*Hell*" staring at the stick in disbelief and consternation. "How in heaven's name! . . . ? We *can't* have used all that in an hour's chugging. We have, though."

"A leak in the tank?"

"I'll say! It must be leaking like Niagara. Thank goodness, Walt always keeps an emergency can in his tackle locker or we'd be properly up the spout."

The little boat was tipping wildly by now as larger waves began to hit the cliff. Toby scrambled forward, opened a locker in the bows, and began tossing out a miscellaneous tangle of stuff.

"It must be somewhere in behind this lot. That's funny, it's usually right in front. . . ."

It was at this moment that I felt the first cold prod of fear—that curious pang, mixed with disbelief in which one tries to duck the likelihood of danger: this can't be happening to *me*. This can't be real.

The boat bumped against a rock.

"I say," Toby called, "shove her off a bit farther, can you? Or, wait, I'll do it; you have a hunt, see if you can find the gas."

He clambered back, bringing with him a single scull that had been lying on the bottom boards, and began manipulating it over the stern of the boat, gradually working us out from the cliff. I noticed that we were, at the same time, drifting rapidly down the coast. There was something rather fascinating about the speed with which the jagged rocks slid by. . . . I turned my eyes from them resolutely and set to hunting through all the nooks and crannies in the boat.

"Well," Toby said five minutes later. "Let's have it? No gas on board?"

I nodded miserably. In a way, I felt worse for him than I did for myself. It was his excursion, his idea, his responsibility. . . . And his face betrayed the agony of self-accusation he was going through.

"Oh, lord, I'm such a *fool*. I could murder myself! How could I not have checked the spare tank? But Walt *always* keeps it on board. I've never known it to be missing before. And a leak as well—it really is most extraordinary—and of all the times it could have happened, it had to be when you were with me. . . ."

"Don't, Toby! Please don't blame yourself. It could have happened to anybody. It certainly isn't your fault. And it doesn't matter—we'll be all right, won't we? Can we row back?"

"Not sculling over the stern like this," he said grimly. "The tide will carry us the other way twice as fast. We'd better concentrate on hoping we'll be seen and picked up. Lucky it won't be dark for a couple of hours yet. Have you anything white? Oh yes, your towel, that's fine. Well, you wave it, and I'll work at keeping us out from the cliffs, they're our main worry."

I felt like a fool waving a towel at nothing, for the benefit of the mocking gulls it seemed, but Toby's dogged work with the scull shamed me; I waved and waved with aching arms.

I thought how George would be behaving in this situation. Of course, it was almost inconceivable that George would find himself in a boat that had run out of gas. Things like that simply didn't happen to him, because he invariably paid for the very best service that money could buy and made sure he got it. George, in such a plight, would have flown into a fury and blamed everybody within range. Which wouldn't have helped a great deal, I reflected, specially as the only person within range was me. Toby seemed a much easier person to be a castaway with.

"You're an angel to take this so calmly," he said, "I should think most girls would be raising cain."

"Oh, I'm sure it makes a therapeutic change from my imaginary nightmares; probably, just what I need." I hoped my voice didn't sound as shaky as I was beginning to feel. How much longer would I be able to go on waving the towel? What would happen when darkness came? Toby had brought a torch, for the cave, but its beam had been somewhat faint and flickering; plainly, the battery was on its last legs.

I thought of Hodge, shut in my room back at the inn. . . .

"One thing," Toby said. "Several people knew we were coming this way, Nab, and Uncle Mark, and Walt. By and by, they'll begin to wonder why we aren't back. Walt may want his boat. I'm really surprised he didn't know about the state of the tank."

Coldly, a thought slipped into my mind. Perhaps, he *had* known? Or perhaps, somebody else had known, somebody who quietly removed the spare gas tank? Half a dozen dinghies were moored together down below the harbor wall; it would be a simple matter to slip from one to another, out of sight.

I didn't say anything of this to Toby. I concentrated on waving my towel.

Half an hour went by.

It was beginning to get fairly chilly. Whitecaps were creaming over the tops of the waves. Nab had said it was raring up for a blow, I remembered. The coast looked a long way off.

"The current's carrying us out. It's really better this way," Toby said, answering my unspoken question when I looked at him. "This is quite a steady little tub, really. We're safer well out to sea than being smacked up against the cliffs."

"I see." Drawing on years of experience, carefully conducted conversations with Father, I did my best to make my tone nicely detached and approving.

Toby suddenly grinned at me, pushing back the forelock that kept falling over his forehead as he sculled. His eyes danced, in spite of the lines of strain round them; momentarily, he looked years younger.

"Meg," he said. He cleared his throat. "Meg, do you know that you are an utter darling? If I had to make a choice of The Girl I Would Soonest Be Washed Out to Sea in an Open Boat With—"

"Hush a moment—listen! Wasn't that the sound of an engine?"

We both listened hard, straining our ears.

"Shout," said Toby.

We released our tensions in a prolonged yell. I waved my towel as if I were a finalist in the all-European towel-waving championships. We drifted. . . .

"All right, all right!" said a chiding voice. "I bain't deaf, nor blind neether. Ben a-following ye this half hour, and a pesky dance ye've led me!"

A little blue boat buzzed up alongside us like a disapproving bluebottle, and a painter whistled between us. "Look alive, now!"

"Nab! Am I glad to see you!"

"Well, take a-hold, then, Master Toby, don't-ee

sit there gawping like a goony!" Nab, the postman, said tartly. "Fair and far off from my lobster pots ye've fetched me, and a proper long pull we're going to have back. I'm surprised at you, boy, I surely am, taking the young lady on such a boggart's jaunt! Here, then, catch a-hold o' these here oars and start pulling—ye needn't think my poor old donkey engine's going to have all the work of fetching ye back."

"WELL," TOBY SAID AS WE FINALLY CHUGGED INTO PEN-leggan harbor, "we're not much later than we planned to be, thanks to Nab."

He took my arm to help me up on to the causeway. I was glad of his support; I felt chilled and absurdly weak.

By now, the wind was quite brisk; hazy clouds were massing together in the west, taking on a red, angry tinge, and the sea birds were crying and whirling in distracted flight.

"End of the fine weather, I fancy," Toby said. "You'll be glad, in the pouring rain tomorrow, that you followed everyone's advice and went back to London."

A large black car was climbing the steep track that led up to the Trevelyan house.

"That's Minkins," Toby said. I could hear the smile in his voice again. "On his way back, doubtless, from laying in delicacies for your meal tonight. Uncle Mark mostly lives on eggs."

"Who's Minkins?"

"Mark's chauffeur-butler-major domo—he's been there forever. Funny old guy. He and Mark are as thick as thieves."

100

Mr. Vosper was on the lookout for us at the pub. Before Toby could start explaining about the gas tank, he said to me, "Oh, miss, a telegram came for you, ten minutes ago. And, Mr. Toby, Mr. Minkins just came down with a message for you—a phone call from your office. They've had a bad fire at the Saltash foundry, and can you go back today, as soon as possible?"

"Oh lord," said Toby. "That's torn it. A bad fire? How the dickens did that happen? Yes, I'll have to go. I'd better nip up to Uncle Mark's and collect my gear."

"Mr. Minkins anticipated that," said Mr. Vosper. "He brought your case down. It's in the car already."

"Oh. Thanks. Very obliging of him. I hope your wire's not bad news?" Toby said to me.

"Not exactly." I looked again at the paper trembling between my fingers. George's wire said:

What the devil do you think you're up to at the back of beyond? Are you coming back or do I have to fetch you?

Not a conciliating message. Evidently he had broken through Venetia's defenses, but equally evident was that he had received some scratches on the way. As I said, even at the beginning, Venetia was not wholeheartedly in favor of George.

"Well," Toby said, "well, I suppose I'd better be off then. I'm very sorry I'll have to miss seeing you tonight. . . ."

We looked at one another irresolutely.

I had a queer, flat, depressed feeling, as if I had suddenly come to the end of a long, important part of my life. Not at all as if I were parting from a casual stranger whom I had only just met.

"I don't imagine you'll be down this way again? Penleggan seems rather unlucky for you."

"It does, just a little. . . . Do you ever come to London?"

"Hardly ever. I suppose you'll be getting married quite soon?"

"I suppose so. Well, good luck."

"Good luck," he said slowly. "And sorry again about this afternoon." He turned and climbed into his two-seater, seemed to hesitate, then flicked a brief salute and drove off.

I wandered drearily indoors, thinking that I'd better put on something respectable for this tedious dinner party that lay ahead. There didn't, somehow, seem to be much point to it now. What was I to Mark Trevelyan or he to me? I certainly didn't intend to paint his portrait.

I pulled out a dress, the only respectable one I had brought with me. Then, it occurred to me that Hodge wasn't on my bed where I had left him.

"Do you know where my cat is?" I asked Mrs. Vosper.

"No, miss. I remember hearing him cry sometime in the afternoon, but you said not to let him out, so I didn't." She looked faintly smug. "I was just going to feed him when you got back."

Somebody *had* let him out, though; my bedroom door had been open.

Vaguely worried, I dressed rather quickly and spent fifteen minutes in a fruitless patrol of Penleggan's little alleyways, calling and searching. But Hodge was nowhere to be seen, and in the end, politeness decreed that I abandon the search and go to keep my dinner date.

Regardless of possible rats, I left the car with

windows open so Hodge would see it and know I'd not deserted him, and did the climb to Trevelyan House on foot, feeling a weary reluctance and a nagging anxiety which I tried to suppress because it seemed so stupid. Hodge had often been missing before for hours at a time.

But I'll come back early, I thought, pleading the long drive tomorrow.

Of course, Hodge would turn up, though. He'd be on my bed when I got back to the pub. Of course he would.

A DARK, EXPRESSIONLESS MAN LET ME IN—I HAD SEEN him before in the bar at the Trevelyan Arms. Presumably, he was Minkins. I noticed that his pale face was so highly polished that it seemed likely he never needed to shave, just gave his cheeks a rub with a silicone cloth from time to time.

He said, "Mr. Trevelyan's in the garden, madam. I'll take you through."

I was vaguely surprised. A lot of wind had come up by now, and the western sky was all curdled with red cloud; it seemed an odd evening for a delicate man to be sitting out. However, when we had passed through the house (I took in little more than a general impression of age, darkness, stone-flagged floors, and a lot of heavy Jacobean furniture), Minkins led me down steps spanning a series of terraces, each ingeniously protected from the wind by movable plastic screens, and commanding a marvelous view of the coast in both directions.

Below us, on the bottom terrace, I saw a table with glasses and decanters, and somebody sitting in a chaise longue. "There he is, Madam," said Minkins, and left me. I walked on, screwing up my eyes against the sunset glare.

Enclosing the bottom terrace was a wall, and beyond this, over to my right, ran a rocky path; I realized that I was seeing my first evening's walk from another viewpoint and that the Devil's Eggcup must lie immediately below the terrace. This was confirmed by the soaring balls of sea foam which blew up continuously from beyond the wall; tonight, they were all colored pink in the sunset light and looked like some sort of futuristic decorative scheme as they rose and drifted and came to rest on gorse and scrub. It was queer to see them blowing so wildly and yet be completely screened from the wind which made a low, insistent booming as it hit the tops of the plastic screens—an ominous sound like the accompaniments to those films where people keep galloping over the steppes.

Mark Trevelyan was sitting wrapped in downy tartan rugs. He had his face turned away from me, looking at the view; a pair of binoculars lay on the arm of his chair. As I approached I said, "Good evening, Mr. Trevelyan," clearly, in case he was deaf, and because of the hum of the wind.

He turned his head.

Three thoughts hit me at the same moment: first, how *very* well he must take care of himself—he looked spare, dry, but flexible, like a well-preserved mummy; secondly, how alike the two brothers, Gerald and Mark Trevelyan, must have been when they were young. Nobody had mentioned that point. I suppose it was taken for granted by people who had always known them. And lastly, I realized what had been wrong with my drawing of the dream-face.

I hadn't given it a beard. Mark Trevelyan had a neat little beard, white and silky, like the down on a seed pod.

I drew a difficult breath.

"Miss Frazer," he said, and stood up, carefully disentangling the rugs. "How kind of you to visit me in my hermitage. I hope you didn't mind coming out here? Toby's screens are quite effective in cutting off the wind, don't you find? And it was only right to let you see the view. I'm so sorry Toby was called away. But Miss Pentecost will be here presently. She paints in water colors, I believe—I am afraid she is the nearest to a colleague that our quiet little village can offer. But I hope that you are finding your stay enjoyable? Toby, I believe, took you on some excursion this afternoon." He looked gently amused.

"I—yes, thank you," I said mechanically. I couldn't take my eyes off his face. This, then, was the simple explanation. This was why I had seen the face first in the rocking chair and then—I remembered it all, now—*above me*, the same face, looking in at the window. But with such an expression! No words, just the two puppet faces, staring, and then the hideous, deafening blast of sound.

I let the silence go on for too long.

"Oh dear," said Mark Trevelyan very gently. "Do you know, I was afraid that something like this might happen? What a great, great pity it was that you had to come back! And that neither of my little warnings took effect."

I never even thought of trying to deceive him.

105

I couldn't have done it, anyway. I'm no actress. And I was curious, too. The terror hadn't taken hold, yet. This place, with its open levels of ground, its great view, the humming wind, the red light, the blowing foam all seemed so different from the shut-in darkness of my dream.

"Why did you do it?" I burst out. "Why did you kill your brother? He was a good man! Everybody says so."

"Good?" Mark Trevelyan said distastefully. "I'm afraid I can't agree with you there. He was a vandal—a desecrator. Why, if he'd had his way, by this time Penleggan would be a sort of Blackpool, with factories, and dance halls, and teen-agers—what do they call them? Flower people. *Juke boxes.* Do you honestly think I could have permitted that?"

He thrust up his chin, frowning, and stared at me through half-closed eyes.

"You are a painter, my dear girl, surely you can understand that his ideas were intolerable? Could I let him cover these cliffs, which have belonged to our family for generations, with bungalows and gas pumps? No, there was only one way to solve it. My first try, scuttling his boat, was a failure. A most disastrous failure. The second time, I planned more carefully and shot him, with his own gun, through the window of his cottage. It was unfortunate that *you* were there—I noticed you a second after I had pulled the trigger— but, as it turned out, not fatal; you appeared to be unconscious, and when I learned two days later that you were suffering from amnesia, it was a relief to know that I need take no further action in regard to you.

"I had intended to leave the gun in his hand, of course, to make it seem like suicide, but suddenly seeing you there distracted me. A pity. In his state of health, what would have seemed more probable than a sudden decision to put an end to his useless life?"

Mark Trevelyan had a curious trick of bowing his head a little, first to one side, then to the other as if acknowledging applause or loosening up his throat muscles. He did this now, then looked up at me with his brilliant, little, cold eyes and said again, regretfully, "It was *such* a pity you had to come here. Either time."

Now, fear began to finger at me again, but I said steadily, keeping the whole thing on a level of polite discussion while I wondered how to get away, "I still don't see how you did it. Weren't you supposed to be up at the hospital reading to your aunt?"

Something white beyond him caught my eye; absently, I noticed that it was my portrait of him, slowly drifting along the flagstones. I supposed that Minkins must have taken it from the pub.

"Oh," he said, "it was the simplest thing in the world. I read aloud to my aunt till she dozed off— she *never* lasted awake for more than five minutes. There was a recorded broadcast of mine on the BBC European Service that evening; I'd timed my visit to coincide with it and chosen the same series of poems to read aloud. As soon as the old girl nodded off, I switched on her radio to the broadcast, turned it up loud enough to be heard through the closed door, and popped out of her window—it was a ground floor room. The matron always left her bicycle leaning against the wall outside; I borrowed it and freewheeled down to the quay in no time. I'd put on a cloth cap, and the street was dark so it was most unlikely that I should be recognized. Peddling back uphill was harder work, though luckily Miss Pentecost had a three-speed—a most useful device—and I suffered a slight heart attack when I reached my aunt's room. I just had time to switch off her radio. She thought I was dead when she woke, poor old soul. Naturally, I have taken more care of myself since then, but in many ways that heart attack was all to the good."

"Supposing someone had come into her room while you were out?"

"She never permitted *anyone* to enter while I was reading my poetry to her," he said, shocked. "No, there was no risk of that kind."

He leaned back, puffing out his cheeks with a slight, self-satisfied smile—like a cockatoo preening itself.

"What about the gun? What did you do with that?"

"My aunt had an enormous jigsaw puzzle of the Battle of Waterloo, about a quarter finished. She hardly ever touched it. It lived on a table in her room. For three weeks, the gun lay in the box underneath all the loose pieces. Then, when I was better, I retrieved it one day while she slept, and Minkins disposed of it. Down *there*." He nodded towards the Devil's Eggcup. "In view of all the disconcerting and unexpected circumstances, I consider that I showed remarkable presence of mind, don't you agree?"

There was something crazily fascinating about his complete egocentricity.

"You realize I intend to tell all this to the police?" I said.

He did not seem in the least perturbed.

"I'd a notion that you might take that ridiculous, puritanical line. All the young seem the same—impractical idealists. I'm afraid I find it very tedious. Well, you must do as you think fit, of course, though it seems a lamentable instance of the horse and the stable door."

I turned to begin the long climb up the terraces and he added, lightly and coldly, "But before you do so, perhaps you had better consider the predicament of your cat?"

And he gestured toward the terrace wall.

My blood turned cold as lemon ice. Somehow, I made my way over to the parapet on legs that would hardly hold me and looked down into the Devil's Eggcup.

The inner wall, over to my right, was sheer: spray-washed granite funneled down to the seething, heaving water at the bottom. I was looking straight across at the seaward rim of the Eggcup which, as I have said, was a narrow isthmus of rock covered with turf. From where I stood, I could see right down into the blowhole to the natural arch where the waves burst in, exploding against the inner wall and flinging their foam high into the air. As well as the flying clots of foam there were gulls, swooping and diving at something small and gold-brown, something that huddled halfway across that crumbling, perilous, outer saddle of rock and turf.

"Hodge!" I whispered. "It's my cat! You put him there. Oh, how *could* you? Of all the mean, filthy. . . ."

"*I* didn't put him there, my dear girl." He stroked his beard complacently. "No, such feats are beyond me now, I fear; I was merely the organizing genius."

So, who? Not Toby? No, I thought, Minkins, of course. Minkins.

"I'm going to telephone the police," I said. "They'll come—they'll bring—"

"Oh, my dear child. I doubt if Minkins will let you. Besides, I daresay our instrument is out of order. And in any case, by the time they got here . . .

I am a very accurate shot with a pebble. Even better than with a gun."

He worked out a loose stone from the top of the wall and hurled it across the blowhole. It passed a foot above Hodge, who flattened in terror and clung to the turf.

"You see? I practice on the gulls, I can assure you I am a prime shot," he said, and laughed.

At that, rage really gushed up in me, like milk boiling over in a saucepan. Childishly, I grabbed a handful of anything I could snatch up off the top of the wall—it was mostly earth—and flung it in his face.

"Damn you!" I shouted. "I won't *let* you kill my cat."

He took a pace back, exclaiming furiously, trying to shake the stuff out of his eyes. In the same moment, I was over the wall and clambering round to the lip of the blowhole. It wasn't till I had reached the seaward side and was beginning a cautious descent backwards down the grass slope to the saddle that I realized what a crazy thing I was doing.

Below me, on my right, was a vertical drop to the sea: sixty feet of cliff. On the left was the blowhole, nearly as deep. Glancing backward over my shoulder, I could see Hodge, crouching in terror as the gulls dive-bombed him. I shouted at them—I dared not wave—and they sheered off. But supposing Hodge panicked and struggled when I tried to pick him up?

I had to make the attempt, though. I wasn't going to leave Hodge, old Hodge, my lifelong friend, comforter of all those unhappy childish nights, to a lonely dreadful death. If I deserted him in such a pass, I'd never be able to live easily with myself again.

"Hodge!" I called. "Hodge puss, it's me." Could he hear me above the wind? I saw his pink mouth open in a soundless cry for help. But he didn't move; he seemed paralyzed with fright.

What would happen if I managed to reach him? What was Mark Trevelyan doing? Would he ever give me a chance to climb back? I was pretty tired already; my arms still ached from waving for help in the boat. Could I haul myself and Hodge back up this break-neck slope?

No use thinking ahead. By now, I had kicked off my shoes and was on hands and knees. I worked myself back another couple of feet, pivoted, and found myself within reach of Hodge. He didn't stir, I don't know if he even recognized me. I laid a cautious hand on him, stroking and soothing. He was completely rigid with fright. I grabbed hold of the loose skin on his shoulders and hauled him up, all anyhow, until I could grip him against me with my left arm. He kicked wildly then, for a moment, but subsided against me, too terrified to struggle any more. I could feel his heart beating against me like the rattle of typewriter keys.

I began on two knees and one hand, to push myself back up the slope. As I did so, a stone struck me viciously on the right wrist, unbalancing me so that I swayed for a moment and almost dropped Hodge. Another sang past my head. Looking up, I saw Mark Trevelyan's furious white face glaring at me over the wall, his hand poised to hurl another stone.

What about his heart condition, I thought. Surely he can't keep this up for long? Or isn't it as bad as he makes out? Then, past him, I caught a glimpse of another figure running down the terrace steps. That was when I really gave up hope. Minkins, of course. It must have been Minkins who kidnapped Hodge when he drove down to the village for supplies, Minkins who spiked the gas tank, no doubt, and put the rat in my

111

car, who was obviously prepared to abet his employer in every way.

Two stones struck my back, and one just missed my face. Uncle Mark was getting his eye in now. With Minkins to help him, I'd soon be done for. And nothing to prove it wasn't an accident. Then I heard a shout.

"Meg! Hang on, I'm coming!"

I lifted my face from the turf and looked up. Unbelievably, it was not Minkins but Toby on the terrace by his uncle. He picked up something—a cushion? I saw his arm flash as he dealt his uncle a violent blow. Mark Trevelyan disappeared.

Then Toby was over the wall and working his way round to the end of the saddle.

"You *crazy* girl!" he shouted. "For heaven's sake, what's going on? How did he get you there?"

He flung himself flat and reached a hand to pull me up, then saw Hodge. "Oh, my God, I see. The cat. . . . Have you got me? Right. Easy does it. . . ."

Half hauling, half supporting, he guided me up to the wall. I was vaguely surprised that the barrage of stones had stopped till I clambered limply over the parapet on to the terrace and saw Mark Trevelyan lying back, half off the chaise longue, his face a curious tinge of blue.

"I believe I've done for him," Toby panted, "and I'm not a bit sorry. We'd better go up to the house and phone. Can you walk? Did he hurt you?"

"No, not too bad. I'll be all right." I tucked Hodge into my arms more firmly. His heart was still thumping nineteen to the dozen.

Then I asked, "What made you come back?"

"I began to be a bit uneasy," Toby said, urging me up the steps. "Really, I was a prize fool not to have guessed long ago. Well—in a way, I suppose I *did* guess, all along—maybe everybody here did. Mark isn't all that keen on strangers as a rule. It seemed funny that he was so anxious to meet you. Then, at Bodmin, I had a flat tire and rang the foundry to say I'd be late. They were surprised; said they hadn't asked me to come. So then I really did get the wind up. I thought about the leaky tank in Walt's boat and it all seemed to add up. I came racing back to Penleggan. Good lord, there's Miss Pentecost."

The little, dumpy woman was approaching us down the terrace. She began, "I'm slightly earlier than I was invited. . . ." then she took a look at me and said calmly, "Shock. Hot sweet tea. Toby, run and put a kettle on. Minkins, for some extraordinary reason, is out; he passed me driving down to the village at a disgracefully fast speed. Forgot the vegetables, I suppose."

I was quite speechless. Miss Pentecost led me into the house, put me on a sofa by a fire, and even produced milk for Hodge. He gulped down two saucersful then climbed onto my lap and stayed there. I lay back; I was in a sort of daze, temporarily. I heard Miss Pentecost and Toby conferring in low tones:

"Yes, his heart. Just as well. Doctor? Rumbold, at St. Kew. Phone out of order? Minkins seems to have cut the wire? How very peculiar. Watching through fieldglasses? Oh, explain later. Your car? My car."

Presently, I heard the sound of a car starting, and Miss Pentecost came to sit by me, remarking, "Toby has just gone to get the doctor. I'm afraid it's too late for Mr. Trevelyan. His heart, you know. Now—have a cup of this really excellent tea. I shall, too."

While I drank it, she produced a flowered knitting bag and began clicking needles in a soothing way.

"Do you want to talk about what happened?" she said.

"Yes, please."

I was still limp with reaction; the story poured out of me. Miss Pentecost listened, knitted, and nodded. Finally, she said, "Of course, I ought to have worked it out long ago. I always wondered who borrowed my bicycle that evening and put it back the wrong way round. Well . . . I don't see a great deal of point in informing the police now, do you? Shall we agree to forget the whole thing? It would be far less distressing for Toby."

"Oh, yes." But then I remembered Uncle Mark's abettor. "What about Minkins, though?"

"Let's leave it to Toby," Miss Pentecost said comfortably. "He's the proper person to decide." And, in fact, I later heard that Toby, finding Mark Trevelyan's desk ransacked, asked the police to put out a call for Minkins; he was picked up at Heathrow with a briefcase full of stolen bearer bonds worth £10,000. "Here's Toby back now, I do believe," went on Miss Pentecost, who had remarkably sharp ears for her age. "He is a good, reliable boy. Now, if you are feeling better, I suggest that he take you down to the inn while I do the explaining to Dr. Rumbold. No need for you to wait about and distress yourself. All right now, my dear? Splendid. Well, I'm delighted to have met you again. No doubt we shall be seeing each other some other time. I should be sorry to miss the chance of our talk about art. Besides, you haven't yet tasted my elderberry wine, which is particularly good this year."

And the remarkable little woman trotted out, calm and unflustered. A moment later, I saw her through the window, talking earnestly to the doctor as she led him down the terrace steps.

Toby came in. He looked pale and shocked.

"I'll run you down to the pub, now, shall I? You won't want to stay here. . . ."

"Thanks," I said awkwardly. "If you wouldn't mind. I still feel a bit. . . ."

"*Don't!*"

He looked at me indecisively, hesitated, then crossing the room in two steps, he dropped down beside me and wrapped his arms round me, suffocatingly tight, pouring out a stream of words. His mouth was muffled in my hair, and my heart had begun thumping so loud that I could hardly hear what he said, "Oh, Meg—when I saw you down there I never—I thought —on that damned bit of rock—last thing I expected— after everything that's happened today I don't suppose you'd ever—but you're the only girl. . . ." And then clearly, "If you'd gone over, I'd have jumped over, too."

We stared at one another, shaken. Then Toby leaned forward and kissed me on the mouth.

"That's forever," he said.

I nodded, mistrusting my voice.

"Do you feel the same way?" he asked.

I nodded again.

"That's all right, then," said Toby soberly. "I had to be sure. Now I'll take you down."

He led me out to his car with an arm round me while I held Hodge. We held hands all the way down the hill.

By now, it was nearly dark. The dim little streetlights faintly illuminated Penleggan quay, the drooping ash tree, and the empty, little white house. Toby drew up in front of the pub.

"I'll have to go back now," he said. "To help with things. I expect Minkins has hopped it. But I'll come down again later—shall I? To see how you are?"

"Yes, please, Toby."

He held my hand tightly in both his for a moment longer, then got back into his two-seater and roared away up the slope.

Hoisting Hodge firmly into my arms, I went into the pub, my mind already at work on the long and difficult task of composing a letter to George.